Supernatural P.I.

A Fawn Malero Adventure

Courtney Davis

DX VAROS PUBLISHING

Published by:
DX Varos Publishing
7665 E. Eastman Ave. #B101
Denver, CO 80231

Book cover design and layout by, Ellie Bockert Augsburger of Creative Digital Studios.

www.CreativeDigitalStudios.com

ISBN: 978-1-955065-62-7 (paperback)
ISBN: 978-1-955065-63-4 (ebook)

To my husband, I know this one is your favorite and I hope that you're not the only one who thinks it's great. I wouldn't have had the confidence to keep writing if you didn't give me such rave reviews along with your constructive criticisms.

Chapter 1

I walked up to the prison with a spring in my step, excited to embark on my first official witness interview as self-appointed Supernatural P.I. for the Seattle area. I wasn't working alone, of course. I had a Werewolf partner and a few quirky supernatural sidekicks I'd collected during my first few mysteries. But this was something I had to do alone. I was nervous and I was excited! I was going to interview a serial killer in training, who I went on one bad date with, and I was instrumental in bringing down. A human who I now needed essential information from. Hopefully, he didn't hold his arrest and incarceration against me.

I couldn't wait to bring some evidence to my father and prove to my brothers that I was more than capable of this job. I imagined soon I would have a belt with handcuffs, stun gun and whatever else a

P.I. might need, like maybe a notepad or some mints? A camera would be good, something small and very spy like. What else did a supernatural private investigator need? Probably a client, I was taking on this first case for myself. Well, for the good of the world really, not that any human or most supernaturals would ever know. My father would, and I could even charge him for the service! It *was* his job to keep order around here and someone had sold a magical book on raising the dead to a human. A very creepy human. I tried not to focus too hard on the fact that I was also hoping to earn his respect and blessing when I solved this. I tried extremely hard to be an independent woman, but that didn't mean I didn't want other people to believe in me too.

My family were Magicians, a supernatural species that held certain abilities. Mine were communicating with animals, super bendability, a little healing, and a supernatural empathic drive to help other supernaturals, and animals. Curiously, it didn't extend to humans for whatever reason. I had to assume it was because their capacity for empathy had been long ago set aside for selfish gains. My powers were so wrapped up in my emotional desire to save that it required an answering empathy to trigger.

I entered the prison and felt a chill run down my spine. The very final click of the door behind me almost made me want to turn and run even though I knew it wasn't locked, this was just the reception area that was open to the public. I walked to the front desk and smiled brightly, hoping my large black eyes were showing none of the nervousness I felt. I had chosen to wear jeans and a red blouse that was low cut, my light brown hair was tied up in a high ponytail with a red ribbon. My goal had been wholesome, and I think I hit it on the head judging by the welcoming smile from the man behind the counter.

"I'm here to speak with Ben Benson." I tried to sound light but internally I was cringing. I couldn't believe I was about to talk to that psycho again. The last time I saw him he was squirming under Logan's enormous Werewolf paws, his dead mother was sitting in the living room in front of a game show, and he had a pet dissection and reanimation lab set up in his basement. I had no interest in ever looking at that human again, but here I was, because I needed information.

"Fawn Malero?" he asked.

I nodded, hoping he wouldn't ask too many questions.

"Okay, you're on the list, follow me," the officer said. "You're his girlfriend?"

"Former, I just want to talk to him one more time. I feel like I need closure."

"This one's a real weirdo, I suppose you didn't know that when you dated him. I can imagine it was shocking when you found out what he was doing in his mom's basement," he looked at me expectantly and I wondered if he wanted details.

"Very," I said truthfully. I really hadn't thought Ben was capable of such things. We had been in Veterinary school together and went on one mediocre date, but I never would have pegged him for serial killer in training. Logan said I had terrible taste in men, which was probably true. I had decided after Ben that I would not be dating humans anymore. Not that I had better luck with supernaturals. The last one I had gone on a date with other than Logan was apparently the one who sold Ben the magical book on reanimating corpses he was trying to use on the animals in his basement, and his mother. Then there was the nurse living in my house who I thought I was falling in love with, well he was running from his ex-coven because he had killed his wife's lover.

"I bet he'll be moved to the psychiatric facility soon," the officer said, breaking me out of my thoughts.

"Yeah, I suppose so." Which is one reason I was here now, I wanted to talk to him before they started giving him drugs to forget his insanity, or shock therapy. Maybe a lobotomy!

Selling magical items to humans was a big offense in the supernatural world and if I could get some lead as to how Ben had contacted Stefan to buy the stuff, we could hopefully stop Stefan from causing any more problems. It was rule number one, don't let humans find out about supernaturals. They were far too dangerous, unpredictable, and given to fits of hysteria. Ben was our best source right now. Stefan was a Magician from New Orleans who owned a magic shop with his sister that apparently sold more than just card tricks.

I followed the officer as he spouted off rules and restrictions, I didn't care to pay attention to. I was a Magician on a mission and Annabel had spelled me before I left the house to make me completely forgettable. When a human was out of eyesight for more than five minutes, the memory of me would completely fade. Might come in handy, I didn't really want Ben to remember what I was prepared to say to him to get the information I needed. Another reason that I had left Logan in the car.

Logan and I had formed this unofficial private investigation business for supernaturals after finding out that we work well together, and damnit, I was pretty sure I was in love with him. It had taken a lot of negotiating to get him to stay behind for this meeting, but there was no way I could get Ben to trust me if Logan were sitting there glaring and growling.

"Wait in booth three, he'll be brought in shortly. Pick up the phone, no touching the glass," the officer reminded.

"Yes, thank you, Sir." I sat down in booth three trying to ignore the conversations going on around me. Supernatural hearing made it easy to eavesdrop. One couple was arguing about their children, one was discussing money problems, and another was talking about who cheated with who. Apparently, the main culprit was the one behind bars and most of the cheating has occurred since he was brought in!

I couldn't hold back a smile, those two had more problems than they wanted to admit.

After about five minutes, Ben was led to the seat in shackles and an orange jumpsuit. He looked smaller, frailer than I remembered, and I wondered if he would survive much longer in there. He had shaved his head, not a big loss, his brown hair had been nothing great. His brown eyes were wide behind his glasses. I didn't recognize the glasses, I guess he used to wear contacts. He picked up the phone and I followed suit.

"Hello, Ben. It's nice to see you," I said with what I hoped was a friendly smile.

"Fawn? This is unexpected, I didn't think I would ever see you again. Not after th-the dog attack," he said nervously.

I took a deep breath preparing for what I had to do. "Well, Ben, I just couldn't get you out of my mind. I wanted to make sure you were okay and see if there was anything I could do to help." I leaned forward, letting my low-cut shirt shift slightly, I wasn't above using my figure for information here. "Is there *anything* you need, Ben?"

His eyes shifted down to my exposed skin and I was sure I had him. "I need a ticket out of here, they think I'm crazy."

That was probably because he told the police he'd been attacked by a Werewolf, thankfully when you have your dead mother propped up in the living room no one takes much of anything you say seriously. Otherwise, he probably would've had to be killed already, in order to keep the secret.

"I know you aren't, Benny. I want to get ahold of the man you bought the book from, I think he might

6

be able to help get you out of here. I just don't know how to contact him." I made a pouty face, hoping I could play on his base male instincts. Humans were simple creatures.

"Mr. S? You think he might have something," Ben looked around nervously and whispered into the receiver, "Magical?"

"Yes!" I said with too much excitement. He looked surprised and I worried I was about to lose him. I slid my hand up and down on the receiver in what I really hoped looked mildly suggestive and not completely idiotic. "Anything to help," I said with a wink.

Ben went back to looking at me lustfully. "I found him online, we met in a dark alley, I never even saw his face really."

"How did you find him?" I pressed.

"I was on a message board with people discussing the dark arts and he approached me. He offered me the book on reanimation and an amulet to bring me luck in love," he smiled sheepishly and met my gaze. It took everything I had not to look away. "I had planned to give it to you, but maybe I didn't have to."

"No, I guess you didn't," I said between clenched teeth, and I saw doubt cross his features. I cleared my throat and continued quickly. "I mean, here I am! And I will try to help, just tell me how I can contact Mr. S."

"The only way is through the message board."

"How do I find it?" I pressed again; I could tell he was starting to rethink things. "I wish we didn't

7

have this stupid window between us," I whispered and touched the tip of my tongue to my top lip, hoping I looked sexy, which is not how I felt.

"Oh, me too!" he agreed and reached out to touch the window, gaining a stern warning from a nearby guard.

"Help me to help you, Ben. How can I reach Mr. S?"

"Go to the message board on the International Magic Exchange website. Leave a message there saying you're looking for something to take your magic game to the next level, he will contact you."

I stood quickly. "Thanks Ben, I will let you know what I find out." I walked away without waiting for his goodbye. I had gotten what I needed and, in a few minutes, he would barely remember I was here at all.

I waved to the guard at the front desk as I passed, and he looked at me confused. He'd already forgotten me, that was a good sign.

Logan was leaning against the car waiting for me. His muscles bulging out of a t-shirt and shorts, despite the cool weather. Werewolves ran hot, I really wished I had that problem, the Seattle weather was chilly this time of year. His brown hair was just about long enough to need a trim, a little shaggy around the ears but I kind of liked it, made him look a little wild, which he was. I smiled knowing I had been all over that body many times in our short relationship.

"How did it go?" he asked, looking me up and down with angry concern that made me melt a little bit.

He was a Werewolf, and he was moody, but he mostly wanted to protect the things he cared about. Right now, that was me and I liked that very much. "I'm fine, we met through glass."

Logan frowned. "I hope that didn't mess with Annabel's spell."

Now I frowned, what if Ben remembered that embarrassing display. "I don't think it will matter, even if he does remember I visited," I lied. There was no reason to worry Logan about far fetched possibilities.

Logan rushed me into the car. "That depends on what you told him."

"I told him that I can't wait to ride him all night long as soon as I can magically help him escape prison," I said monotone and raised an eyebrow sarcastically.

Logan growled and slammed my door. He hurried around and got into the driver's seat, gripping the steering wheel white knuckled. "I know you're joking, but don't. It is way too close to the full moon for me to even think of you with someone else."

"Territorial Werewolf," I teased, leaning over and kissing him.

"Yes," he grunted. "Where to now?" He said gruffly.

"I told your sister we would stop by the bar for a drink, Drake and Zin are meeting us there." Logan's sister, Lila, owned a bar in my territory. It was a place that all the supernaturals liked to mingle and hang at and recently had become one of my favorite places to spend the evening.

"Oh yeah, and Betina?"

"She went to see a band with Chase." My littlest brother had taken my ward under his wing, which was really nice for me. Betina was a teenage Troll and needed constant attention and activity. She had been living a terrible life underground with her parents, even for a Troll it had been bad. She was the daughter of their leader in this area, but she didn't look like them, was considered ugly by them! She looked a lot like a human actually. She was very tall and broad but not like most Trolls, which were enormous and never could pass for human. They had bulbous noses, enormous eyes that were like wet black pools of sadness. They didn't care to cover their gnarly hairy feet and their best defense mechanism was smell, oh man, the smell they could emit! Like vomit and rotten fish. But Betina had a small nose, large black eyes, a lot like mine actually and short brown hair that had a nice shine but nothing like the wet look most Trolls had. I was sure she wasn't full Troll, no matter what her mother said, who also didn't look full Troll. Betina's twin brother was very Troll like and disgusting, he was currently in trouble for selling psychedelic sludge to Vampires.

Betina had turned out to be a sweet girl, given to fits of teenage antics at times, she had also become essential to my yoga studio. Now a trained instructor working nights with Zin, Logan's adopted Vampire sister, providing classes to the supernaturals in the area. My business had never done better! Who would have thought a 24-hour yoga studio would do so well!

I looked over at Logan and smiled. It was really only because of him that I had all this. All these friends and a thriving business that catered to humans and supernaturals. He'd come along and forced me to recognize my rightful place as part of this world. Instead of the one I'd been idolizing for so long after my isolated years growing up watching humans on television.

"What?" He asked skeptically at my staring.

"I was just thinking about how lucky I am to have you around, forcing me to do dangerous things like talk to a psycho human in prison."

Logan huffed and rolled his eyes. If he'd had it his way, he would have been the one to go in today. I laughed.

Chapter 2

We pulled up to *Brews for Beasts* as the sun went down and it looked packed, of course it *was* a Friday night. I never would have thought I would so enjoy a night surrounded by so many different supernaturals, drinking and dancing. My parents had known that I had a natural empathetic power and they had thought it best to keep me away from those who might trigger that part of my powers. So I never got very comfortable with it, I still wasn't fully there, but willingly working on it.

"Fawn!" Lila called from behind the bar, shooing away a couple of Vampires who were chatting her up. "I am so glad you guys stopped by." Lila was one of my best friends. She was a typical Werewolf female, wide shoulders, large breasts, dark hair, and eyes. She was very pretty, extremely sweet, and very tough.

"Of course," I said. "Its Friday night and I wouldn't want to be anywhere else." I looked around the room briefly, assessing. There were Vampires, Werewolves, Witches, and a couple Trolls. All mixing and mingling happily, a couple of months ago I wouldn't have believed a place like this existed.

"It's happening tonight! I'm sure it's the full moon, we always are busy the night before I close," she laughed and handed me a couple beers.

"Thanks."

"So, are you coming to Brakemoor tomorrow?"

I had spent the full moon up there with them once but that was before Logan and I were even actually dating, in fact he had still basically hated me at that point. I wasn't sure how I felt about being there as his date. "I don't know, we haven't really talked about it."

"Well, I think my parents expect it. Logan hasn't kept your relationship a secret." She rolled her eyes. "Bragging really, I think he wanted to make sure no other Werewolf even thought about approaching you for a date."

I looked over at him, waiting and watching me carefully from the table. I appreciated that he wasn't ashamed of our relationship, but I also wasn't sure I was ready to be inducted into the Werewolf pack just yet. "Oh, well, I guess we'll see. I might have some stuff to do."

"Oh yeah! Did you get a lead today?"

"Kind of, I'll talk to you about it later," I said with a smile and took the beers to the table.

Logan immediately chugged half of it then took a deep breath. "Okay, so tell me all about it."

"We need to get a message to Mr. S apparently. Ben told me to go on a site and leave the message, then I guess we wait for Stefan to respond." I shrugged, it was what Ben said, but it seemed a little too easy. Was Stefan really just hanging around a weird magic website waiting for sad humans to ask for ways to improve their lives?

Logan looked doubtful too. "Stefan isn't an idiot; we need to be very careful."

"I know," I said a little too defensively. "We just have to intrigue him, what could we ask for that he would willingly sell to a human?" We sat silently sipping for a while.

Drake and Zin showed up and joined our table, chattering happily, sipping cups of blood. They were nearly inseparable lately and I wondered how long it would last before Drake was called back by his father or sent out on another mission. He had come here because of some dissent among the Portland youth, he stayed because he loved Zin. She was young and beautiful and so fun. She reminded me of a goth pixie, short black hair and ice blue eyes. She was predictably pale and had a slight figure. She was fascinated by Drake who had the dark brooding Vampire look. He was handsome and tortured, having lost his wife and young child many years ago. Logan worried that Zin was going to break Drake's heart because she was too young to be serious about a relationship. I wasn't so sure, she seemed completely enamored. Of course, I made terrible choices in love so maybe I shouldn't try to guess other's intentions.

"Was your mission successful?" Drake asked.

"It's too early to tell, but I have a lead!" I said excitedly.

"You're going to be a great P.I." Zin laughed. "Fawn Malero, Supernatural P.I." she said dramatically waving her hand like she was reading a sign.

"Maybe Fawn and Logan's Supernatural Investigators," I said.

"What exactly do you think we will be investigating?" Logan said with a laugh. "More like supernatural law enforcers."

I gave him a hard look. "I don't know, you showed up on my doorstep with a problem, so did Xander. Ben, well I'm quite sure you told me to investigate the dead animals that led to him. So now I just need to start charging for my services and it's a business!" Everyone laughed and I frowned.

It wasn't more than ten minutes later that my next mission walked into the bar.

The bar door burst open and a woman walked in, dripping wet, naked, and wrapped in a towel. She looked like she had just crawled out of the sound. There were bits of seaweed dangling from her red hair, she wore a seashell necklace, and her emerald green eyes practically glowed. The entire bar turned to stare at her, she was beautiful and frantic, running across the room, clutching her towel and her bare feet left water marks on the floor. There was an odd sucking sound when she walked that I couldn't explain and as she passed, I was hit with a smell I couldn't at first identify.

"What the hell?" Logan whispered next to me, his eyes were wide, and he was watching the woman as close as anyone else.

I had a moment of jealousy but then saw his nose bunch, he didn't like the smell of her either. It wasn't like the rotten smell of a Troll; it was just unusual. The woman practically threw herself against the bar in front of Lila. Lila's eyes went a little wide, but she was doing a very good job, I thought, of hiding her shock at this woman.

"I am looking for Fawn Malero," the woman said, and Logan growled.

Her voice was surprisingly deep for such a small body and the sound of my name coming out of her mouth was jarring. If I had been drinking at that moment, I probably would have done a spit take. Lila pointed at our table; we were all still staring.

"Traitor," Logan growled at his sister quietly.

I put a hand on Logan's leg, hoping to keep him calm. This woman definitely didn't look dangerous, and she certainly looked like she needed help. I could already feel something inside me waking up, my need to help a helpless creature activating. I stood as she hurried over, "I am Fawn, what can I do for you?" The rest of the bar seemed to still be listening though many were now being more subtle about it.

"I need your help, Fawn," she said looking around nervously. "I am Eldoris, I was sent to find you." Her peculiar scent was strong now and I felt like I had smelled it before, maybe this type of creature had been around my father's house at some point when I was growing up.

"Why don't you have a seat, Logan see if Lila has some clothes this poor woman can borrow." I motioned for Eldoris to take my seat and gave Logan a pointed look. He frowned but left to do as I asked. "Can we get you something to eat? Or Drink?"

"No, thank you." She took my seat and I sat in Logan's.

We were secluded enough that a whisper wouldn't be readily heard over the loud music that Lila had thoughtfully just turned up. I looked at the woman and smiled, I noticed now that she had a strange pattern to her skin along her inner arms and palms, her fingers were longer than normal and as she touched the table, I heard that slight sucking sound again. I was beyond confused, what the hell was she?

"I came out to find you," she said a little frantic still. "I didn't know who else to come to for help, we are all suffering."

"Who? Suffering what?" I asked, deeply concerned.

Eldoris looked around, nervously.

"Who told you to find Fawn?" Drake asked quietly.

"Fanlin," she said simply.

"The Elf?" I said incredulous. Fanlin was the leader of the Water Elf clan that was technically part of my father's territory, however they kept very separate and lived northwest of Seattle, farther out on the Olympic Peninsula near the water.

"Yes, Fanlin and his clan are caretakers of the ocean and he told us that you were the one to speak to here about what's happening." She was speaking quietly now.

"What exactly is happening?" Logan asked, handing her a pile of clothes.

"Oh, thank you..." she looked around, nervous again. "I'm sorry this was all I could find to cover my body on my way here. I'm not used to being around such prudish creatures as you all are up here." She dropped the towel revealing her completely nude body, much to the delight of many males in the room. Her stomach and chest were covered in the same odd circular pattern I had noticed on her arms and palms. Drake and Zin moved fast, putting themselves between her and the crowd even as a few brave males moved closer. Logan rushed to grab the towel and held it up to give her a little cover, not that she seemed to care. "How do I work this?" she said holding up a t-shirt. I tried to hold back my frustration as I grabbed it from her and pulled it down over her head. "Oh neat!" she giggled, smoothing it over her body, her wet hair immediately soaked the thin material which clung to her in a very revealing way.

This was not going to work. I handed her the leggings. "Pants, like this." I mimed putting on pants, I was *not* going to do that one for her.

"Fun!" she said, pulling up one leg and then the other and ending with a loud snap as the stretchy material hit her stomach. "I can't believe I am

19

wearing clothes like you guys!" She twirled and lifted one leg then the other.

"You are causing quite a stir, maybe we should go somewhere more private to talk?" I suggested.

"Oh yes," she agreed.

We waved to Lila and hurried out. "Logan, you jump in with Drake and Zin, I'll take Eldoris in my car." My car had a back seat, but it was very small and it wasn't really worth using if it wasn't necessary.

Logan growled, clutching my keys. "I don't like it; we don't even know what she *is!*" he whispered.

I looked at the girl, barefoot and obviously scared. She was of no danger to anyone, I was sure. There was an air of lightness about her, as if she weren't as thick as she seemed and she *seemed* pretty damn thin. Maybe she was an illusion, or a ghost of some sort. "Logan, it will be fine. I'll see you guys back at the house." I gave him a quick kiss and opened the car door for Eldoris.

"A car! Oh my, wait till I tell everyone I rode in a car!" She got in gleefully and I couldn't help laughing. Whatever she was, it was going to be interesting knowing her.

"She can't be real," Logan said as he opened my door for me.

"But I think she is," I hopped in the car and sped out of the lot, Drake's truck following close behind.

"So where are we going?" Eldoris asked. She rolled the window down and put an arm out, riding the wave of wind like a child often does.

"We are going to my house; we will be safe there to discuss whatever it is you came here to get help for." And on the off chance she was nuts, well it was a good place to hold her safely captive. My basement was outfitted with an unbreakable cell in the basement. Made by my father. One of his powers was to forge metal that was unbreakable by anyone, human or supernatural.

"Cool, and I can trust the others? I was told to talk to you... but I know Logan is the son of the Werewolf leader, seems trustworthy. Fanlin mentioned he might be with you. What about the others?"

"Zin is a Vampire that Logan's family found as an infant and adopted, she is young, but she is definitely trustworthy. Drake is a Vampire, son of Cassius Vamprose, definitely trustworthy. Whatever it is you're dealing with, we will do all we can to make sure things are put right. Truth and justice above all else, that is what my father raised me to believe."

"Fanlin certainly believed it, otherwise he wouldn't have sent me to you." She smiled brightly, her emerald eyes sparkling. "Can we listen to music! Isn't there music in cars?"

"Of course." I turned on the radio and blasted my favorite music station that played the best of old rock. Eldoris loved it. She started to move in her seat to Tom Petty and I couldn't help joining in, shouting the lyrics to *Free Fallin*.

Chapter 3

By the time we pulled into my garage I had decided that I really liked Eldoris. "Welcome to my little home."

"Cool!" she jumped out of the car eagerly.

"Oh, a new friend!" Evie said, appearing in the doorway, her ghostly form in a blue suit and tie today, her grey hair pulled back in a tight ponytail.

"Evie what are you wearing?" I asked, trying to hold back a laugh.

"I miss Alfred, so I put on one of his old suits," she said matter-of-factly.

"A real ghost! No way!" Eldoris said excitedly.

"Evie is my roommate, she used to live here with her husband, Alfred."

"That is so cool!" Eldoris walked up to Evie and shoved a hand through her body.

"Rude!" Evie squealed and disappeared.

"Sorry!" Eldoris called out to the air, then turned back to me. "I didn't mean to offend her."

"Don't worry, she never stays mad long. Or out of my business," I grumbled. Evie was a very nosey roommate, and she couldn't leave the house so all her energy was spent focused on me most of the time.

"What is she, other than a ghost I mean."

"Just a human as far as I can tell. What are you?" I asked tactlessly as we walked into the house. Logan, Drake and Zin were walking in through the front door at the same time. Jake and Pete were already wagging tails and waiting for their favorite Werewolf, they barely paid me any attention anymore. Chester, my parakeet tweeted a greeting, happy to see me home.

"I'm a Shifter, my usual form is that of an octopus."

Now the odd pattern and sucking noise made sense. It was her suction cups!

"I've never met a shifting creature of the water," Logan said with amazement, stepping forward to examine her closer. "Is it triggered by anything or completely voluntary?" He was looking her over rather intensely, up and down and all around. I almost wanted to reach out and smack him, but I was confident enough that it was only curiosity driving the inspection. As long as it didn't last too long...

"Like I said, my usual form is that of an octopus. I have spent truly little time in this human form. I can stay in either as long as I like. I am not a *Were* anything, they are controlled by an outside element, a shifter is in complete control of their physical change."

Logan stepped back and I think he was a little jealous, it couldn't be easy to be forced to change once a month. It didn't matter what you wanted to do or not do. Once a month you were lost to the animal for a time. He could shift whenever he wanted, sometimes driven by intense emotions, sometimes just for fun, but the forced moon change was something he could do nothing to avoid.

Fish, fish, fish! Two of my cats, Jasper and Sofia, meowed incessantly as they came into the room. They sniffed at Eldoris' feet and much to my horror began licking at her toes. "Shoo." I waved them away. They moved, but not far. *Food*, they demanded by their half empty bowl. "Cats, never satisfied."

"They seem to have you well trained," Eldoris said as I fed them.

"Yeah, they're hard to ignore," I admitted. Pumpkin came in next, rubbing against Drake's leg, *friend* she meowed. Pumpkin had sort of adopted Drake when he'd been hurt and passed out in my basement. He was still her favorite. "Let's sit and talk," I said motioning to the living room.

Once we were all settled, Eldoris explained. "It started about a month ago. A weakening among all of the supernaturals in the ocean. It's like something is pulling the power out of the ocean and with it, our life forces. I don't know how long until it's too much, we could all die." She was calm and focused as she told us about how some of the older supernaturals were suffering greatly. It hadn't been as big an impact on the younger generations, but they were still feeling it.

"Do you have any idea what's doing it?" I felt like I should have a notebook, this was a big deal, and she wanted *my* help! Had been recommended to find me even, I had no idea why Fanlin thought I would be helpful, but I was glad he did.

"Yes, can I have a glass of water?" she asked.

"Of course!" I hurried to the kitchen and got her a glass of water like a poor hostess for not offering refreshment first thing, my mother would be ashamed.

"Thank you." She took the glass and set it on the table without taking a drink.

"I'm sorry, did you want something else? Saltwater or?" I was confused, I did *try* to be a good hostess.

"Oh, no, thank you," she said and started to wiggle her fingers around the top of the glass. I thought for a moment she was nuts but then the water started to move. It lifted up and swirled around, forming something. "There is a legend that says a stone was stolen from Poseidon himself and taken into the world of men. It has the power to control everything within the sea, but its power comes from the ocean itself and with every use, it takes as much as it gives. It must be returned to the sea." The water had moved and taken shape while she spoke and floating in the air was the image of a large stone, maybe the size of a golf ball.

"What color is it?" Zin asked.

"That color," she said simply, pointing to the water, then looked at Zin and cocked her head. "Or like your eyes almost, maybe a little lighter."

"You think its being used to drain the power out of the ocean? By whom? Why?" I asked.

"Yes, it's the only thing in our legends that could do such a thing. As to why or who, I don't know. That's what I need you to find out."

"Fawn Malero, Supernatural P.I. at your service," I said proudly.

"Fawn and Logan," Logan corrected.

"Yes," I said patting his leg. "Logan and I are partners, so you get two great minds working on this case."

"Wonderful, where do we start?" Eldoris asked.

It was a good question and I had just one thought, "Mr. S."

"Who the hell is Mr. S?" Zin asked.

"We think it's Stefan selling magical items to humans, its what Ben told me today," I explained, hoping it didn't sound completely ridiculous.

"Great, how do we get ahold of this Mr. S?" Eldoris asked, her eyes wide and hopeful.

"We leave a message on a website and wait for his response." I knew it was not going to be what she wanted to hear, it could take far too long.

"I don't know what a website is, but waiting is not an option, we need to do something now!" Eldoris was suddenly frantic and as she worried, the water in front of her exploded, sending droplets around the room. Jake and Pete barked, Pumpkin got pissed and jumped off Drake's lap. Drake let out

27

a shout as Pumpkin's claws dug into his leg on her way.

"Relax!" I commanded and the animals settled quickly. Eldoris stared at me with wide eyes, looking like she was about to cry. "Sorry, I was talking to the animals. I understand you're upset, Eldoris. You have every right to be, I-*we* will do everything we can to find out who has that stone. Contacting Mr. S won't be our only move." Not that I knew what other move I would be making.

"We have no reason to assume it's a human." Logan pointed out. "What other supernatural would have an interest in harnessing the power of the ocean?"

"It seems all the ocean creatures are being affected equally, and besides, we all know its power belongs to all of us," Eldoris defended. "We don't compete. It has to be a land being who is taking from the ocean."

"Has there been any history of animosity or jealousy that could be motivation for this sort of thing?" Logan asked.

"Not that I know of, what benefit would a Vampire or Werewolf have to take from the ocean supernaturals?" Eldoris shook her head.

"She's right, it doesn't make sense. We may want to talk to the Elves though, they might have noticed something. The Trolls too, they have a connection to the water." Most importantly it would make me feel like I was doing something to solve the problem, because I had no idea what else to do. What if I couldn't solve this fast enough? Eldoris and whatever other supernaturals there were in the ocean were in real danger.

"We can ask around a little tonight, but Vampires have never had any interest in ocean creatures, disgusting blood," Drake said, then looked at Eldoris sheepishly. "Sorry."

"Thanks Drake, maybe someone has heard something, its worth asking. I'll text Betina, send her and Chase to talk to her parents, maybe the Trolls have heard something. Logan, I think you and I should walk the water's edge, see if there's anything out of the ordinary going on."

"I'll join you two," Eldoris said jumping up.

I got a bit of a rush, hot on the trail, working the streets! I grinned at Logan and he rolled his eyes at me. "Okay! Let's do this!" I felt good, I didn't care if he thought I was ridiculous. Maybe I was getting too excited about this but hey, I was taking on this case, and I was taking charge. I had every reason to believe I would solve it. Mostly because I didn't want to think about what would happen otherwise. Entire species going extinct, it was unthinkable.

We parked downtown and walked along the piers, nothing seemed out of the ordinary. There were plenty of people despite the late hour and chill air. Restaurants were still open and so was the Ferris wheel. Street performers were out playing music and selling art. Nothing out of the ordinary.

"Wow! The lights are amazing," Eldoris said as we stood watching the Ferris wheel turn on the pier. "I've seen it from below before but never like this."

"Yes, a favorite of all the visitors to our area for sure," I agreed. I almost suggested she check out the aquarium we'd passed, but then thought better of it, she might not like the idea of all those captive creatures. I'd been through there once, it was pretty bad, most of the smaller creatures didn't realize they weren't at home in the ocean. The larger ones, the seals, the octopus and the otters... they knew, and they cried out for the home they'd been taken from or the one they saw in their dreams. It was excruciating for me to hear.

"So, what is your plan, Eldoris? Are you going back tonight?" Logan asked rather rudely, I gave him a stern look and an elbow to the ribs.

"You are welcome to stay with me until we can resolve this issue," I said quickly.

"Thank you, Fawn. Yes, I was told to stay and see it done." She didn't turn away from the lights as she spoke. "I can't go back empty handed."

Logan scowled and some nearby humans crossed to the other side of the street. "Logan you're making a scene. You look like you want to murder someone," I whispered.

"Aren't Werewolves always grumpy?" Eldoris asked.

"Yes," Logan growled, and I laughed.

"Well, there are times I've seen him smile, but mostly in private," I teased.

Logan growled a deeper, more primal growl, and pulled me in for a quick hard kiss. "Let's get to that then."

"Yeah, I don't see a point in hanging out around here more tonight. I think we need a better plan," I grumbled. It didn't feel good to have no idea where to start and the thought of not being able to help this creature was painful. "We will reflect in the morning."

The drive back to my house was mostly silent. Logan's truck rumbled and leaning against him in the front seat was relaxing. If it weren't for a nagging feeling that I was taking on more than I could handle with this one, I might have been lulled half to sleep. We pulled up to my house and I was disappointed to not see Betina's car out front.

"It doesn't look like Betina has returned, I guess you'll meet her tomorrow." We walked inside and were greeted furiously by Jake and Pete, well, Logan was greeted, Eldoris and I were ignored.

Home! Love! Jake and Pete continued to bark, dissatisfied with the lack of attention. Of course all that love and affection was directed at Logan. I rolled my eyes, the cats hurried forward next, smelling Eldoris' feet meowing *fish*. "My animals have abandoned me," I laughed, then Chester swooped over and landed on my shoulder, tweeting a happy hello. "I guess its just you and me, Chester."

"Don't be offended by dumb animals," Evie said popping in. "They don't know what's good for them."

"Thanks, Evie, was the house quiet while we were out?"

"Very, I was bored so I watched the news. Very boring all about the fishing industry tonight."

"Eldoris is going to be staying with us for a while." I turned to Eldoris a little unsure. "You are welcome to sleep on the cot in the basement or the couch, whichever you prefer." I had no idea what would be best for an Octopus Shifter.

"I would prefer water, if possible, do you have a pool or a large container perhaps?"

"I imagine the bathtub would suit you," Logan offered.

"You young'uns and your weird internet challenges. I heard about one where you lay on stuff, what is fun about laying on stuff!"

I laughed, Evie had her own way of compartmentalizing what happened around her so she didn't have to admit to what she was or what any of the rest of us were. "This way, Eldoris."

"Oh yes, I'll be quite comfortable in here," she said, looking at the tub. "Can I have some salt for the water please."

"Sure. This is the hot and this is the cold, here's the plug." I showed her how to use the tub then I brought her some salt and watched her fill the tub with cold water and dump in the salt. It was all very surreal.

"Is there anything else I can get you?"

"Do you have any shellfish?"

"No, sorry I don't eat animals and Betina and Logan prefer red meat."

"Well, I suppose I can gather some tomorrow. Goodnight Fawn, and thank you for taking this on." She looked at me, her eyes full of sadness and her mouth turned down slightly. "We have to find it."

I smiled, knowing I was going to do everything I could to help this supernatural. It was my calling. "Of course, I just hope I will be able to help. See you in the morning." As I was leaving, I saw her slip one hand into the water, it transformed before my eyes into a long red tentacle. I couldn't help shivering a little, it was definitely creepy and somehow felt intimate to watch. I walked out of the bathroom, closing the door behind me.

"Is she going to sleep in the water?" Evie asked, stationed outside the bathroom door, not caring one bit about privacy.

"Yes, she is more comfortable in her octopus form."

"You have some weird friends, Fawn. In my day, a girl didn't associate with such things."

"In your day people thought cocaine was a great additive to soda."

Evie rolled her eyes and disappeared. I walked to the living room and found Logan on the couch, setting a trap for Mr. S. "How's it going?"

"These people are idiots," he said dryly.

"What people might that be?"

"On this magic website forum. The way they talk, I bet *all* of them are living in their mother's basements."

I couldn't help laughing, sad but true, I was sure. The one I knew who'd been on that site was definitely his mother's basement dweller. "So did you post something cryptic that Mr. S will answer but not see through immediately? Something like,

Werewolf seeking new magical ways to please his woman."

Logan laughed darkly, "As if I need help in that department."

I blushed because it was true, he was damn near perfect in that department.

"I went with; *Single man looking for a way to attract more ladies. Want my magic to really blow their minds and attract their attention. Anyone have anything really amazing to take my magic to the next level?*"

"Sounds perfectly pathetic! I hate that we just have to wait and hope he bites."

"Yeah, fishing has never been my sport either." Logan turned on me fast, pouncing and taking me gently to the ground. "I prefer to stalk, pounce, and devour my prey. Not wasting time waiting for it to bite my hook." He opened his mouth wide and gently trapped my neck, letting his teeth scrape softly against my skin as he pulled back. I shivered.

His eyes were dark with passion as he gazed down at me. So close to the full moon I could see the wolf there pacing, itching to come out. I kissed him and giggled, not at all frightened. "I know! And I appreciate your technique very much."

"You know I have to head to Brakemoor tomorrow." he frowned. "I don't like leaving you alone."

I sighed, he had to leave and spend the full moon with his pack, it was tradition. I couldn't join, not with Eldoris swimming around my bathtub with a huge problem to solve. "I know, and you know that I can't go, right?"

Logan narrowed his eyes. "I don't like the idea of you doing any investigating on your own."

It was my turn to narrow my eyes. "I am not promising anything other than to be careful."

Logan growled and gathered me into his arms. He carried me up the stairs and threw me on the bed. He growled at the cats and they hurried from the room then he shut the door. "Do you know what the impending full moon makes me want to do to you?" His voice was more growly and gruff than usual.

Heat flooded my body, "I can only imagine," I whispered as he stalked toward me, undressing slowly.

"You're going to miss out tomorrow night. The sex after a full moon run is intense, or so I've heard."

I wanted to be jealous thinking of him with someone else, having experienced just that. Perhaps another Werewolf that would have the same high as he did when the full moon was up. Was it something he would miss eventually if we stayed together? I shook my head; those were not the thoughts I wanted to think right now. "I can only imagine." I said a little breathless.

"I guess we'll have to make do with tonight." He jumped and landed on the bed, looming over me with a proper predatory grin.

"Make me sorry I am even thinking of staying behind," I goaded.

He did.

Chapter 4

The next morning Logan was gone, off to Brakemoor to celebrate with his family and pack. Betina reported that the Trolls had noticed a shortage in the fish supply, but nothing magical necessarily. Zin texted before dawn that there was nothing among the Vampires to raise alarm and my brother, Chase wanted me to know that Betina was a *badass*.

"You and Chase had a good time last night?" I asked Betina as she sat in front of the tv, scarfing down cereal.

"Yeah, your brother knows a lot of fun people and they don't even care that I'm a Troll! He introduced me to this guy who runs a boat shop downtown, Tony. We are going to get dinner sometime."

I bristled a little, Betina wasn't my daughter, but I was in charge of her care. "And Tony is a..."

"Warlock, just moved to town," she said with lots of teenage attitude.

I couldn't help picturing Xander. His guilt had been certain, and death was his likely sentence. He was sweet to me when I was hurt, but he was probably just using me. I shook off the hurt at his deception. I tried to focus only on the problem at hand. "And Chase approves?"

"Yep, says he seems nice. Geeze, Fawn why are you so grumpy?" she said around a mouthful of cereal. "Isn't Logan keeping you satisfied," she said with a wink.

I decided to ignore the second remark. "I don't want your parents to think I'm letting you run wild." She just rolled her eyes and went on eating. "Did you meet Eldoris this morning?"

"Yeah, she left, said she had to get breakfast. I gave her directions to the fish market."

I started feeding the cats and froze. "The fish market!"

"Whoa settle down, its not like I sent her to buy crack."

"Evie!" I yelled, she was never around when I wanted her and always there when I didn't. "Evie!"

She appeared behind me in a robe and slippers as if I'd rushed her out of bed. I was fairly sure she didn't sleep, but she did like to dress for the occasion. "What are you yelling about so early in the morning?"

"What was the news saying last night about fishing?"

"What the hell, you interrupted my beauty sleep for that boring story?

"Yes, now what did they say?"

"There was a story about some guy who was making a killing at bringing in fish lately." She said with a feigned yawn.

I bit my lip and clasped my hands in excitement. "I think I know what the stone is being used for!" I couldn't help shouting. "What if a human bought it and is using it to catch more fish! You said that the Trolls have noticed a decrease in fish. The news is talking about a guy who is doing great at fishing! What else could a human want to harness from the ocean?"

"Way to go Magnum, now what?" Betina said.

"You and I are going to the fish market."

"Great, I will put on my rubber boots," Betina grumbled.

When we left, we were both wearing rain boots and jeans, turtlenecks, and rain jackets. I had grabbed a can of pepper spray and stuck it in my pocket, just in case. I didn't relish the idea of carrying any kind of weapon, I always felt like I was more likely to hurt myself than anyone else. But I promised Logan this morning before he left that I would be cautious, so here I was, packing heat against my own good judgement.

"Is that all you're taking with you?" Evie asked.

"What else could I possibly need? We are going to question some humans, not supernaturals. Betina is a good enough weapon for that!"

"Yeah, I won't let anything happen to her, don't worry Evie."

"Ha! A smart-ass teenager, what kind of weapon is that?" Evie scoffed.

"If you could smell, you'd know," I laughed.

Evie huffed and disappeared; she didn't like it when I pointed out that she wasn't alive. I'd just recently realized that she didn't have the ability to smell. I knew she didn't eat or sleep but hadn't ever thought about her sense of smell. Evie was lucky, because when Betina got mad, oh man she really made a stink!

"Do you really think we don't need any real weapons?" Betina asked as we got in the car.

"Like what? A garden shovel? I don't keep weapons." I was stronger than I looked, Logan was teaching me a little bit of self defense, and I was harder to break than a human. I wasn't helpless, but compared to most other supernaturals, I was basically a weak human.

"You might be the worst P.I. ever, Fawn."

"Hey! I'm just getting started, maybe I'll pick up some brass knuckles on the way home."

Betina laughed. "And what, throw them as you run away? Because you hitting someone, oh man, that's just ridiculous."

"Thanks for the vote of confidence. How many times have *you* been in a fist fight?"

"Well never, but I'm not the size of a teenage human girl, you are!"

It was true, I was quite small, but I worked out every day and I could throw around some weight if I had to. Betina was thick, tall, and muscular, I wouldn't want to take her on in a fist fight, that's for sure. But it wasn't all about strength, you had to know what you were doing too, and I'd grown up wrestling around with my brothers, I knew some weak spots.

"So do we have a plan?"

I sighed, the truth was no. "Yeah, we just need to walk around and see what doesn't add up. Someone is bringing in a magically large number of good fish, should be obvious."

"Sounds good to me, I love an adventure!" Her face was bright, her black eyes full of excitement. She was a good partner.

We parked near Pike Street Market and made our way through throngs of people to the fish market. There were plenty of weird people to look at, but this was Seattle, humans felt perfectly safe to be whatever they wanted here. None of them looked like they were secretly sucking the power out of the ocean for their own selfish gain, however.

"Where do we start?" Betina asked, her eyes on a cute young boy with his arms elbow deep in a tub of live crabs.

She wasn't obsessed with Tony the Warlock, which made me happy. Teenage hearts sometimes became too quickly bound and were so easily broken that way. "Let's split up and ask around about big catches, all these booths look about the same," I suggested, there didn't seem to be anything more dangerous than us here.

"Cool, see ya," she said and quickly made her way over to the cute boy.

I watched her go with a smile on my face. Young and open to love. Moments like this made me so thankful I took her in, she'd be suffering alone if I'd left her with her clan.

"I can't believe Logan left you alone." A voice I didn't recognize growled in my ear and what I had to assume was a gun poked into my side. "Make a sound and I shoot that Troll before I drag your ass out of here. I need *you* alive for now, but you don't have to be unharmed."

I wasn't sure what was going on and Betina was highly engaged in her conversation with the fish cutie. I held my hands out to signal I was in agreement. He grabbed my arm and I caught a whiff of him, Werewolf. Cole must have sent someone to kidnap me, or perhaps there was still a group in Portland who were mad we stopped them from gaining followers here to go with their come out to humans plan. Either way, I could be in serious trouble. He led me out of the crowd and to an underground parking area. Alarms were going off in my head, isn't this the dumb blonde move in all those horror movies, going somewhere private with the killer in the hopes that he won't really kill you if you're nice. When we were mostly alone I dared a glance.

"Kyle?" I said, incredulous.

"You were expecting someone else? You piss off a lot of people?"

"Actually, yeah," I laughed, because if I didn't laugh I was sure I would cry. I'm sure P.I.'s were not supposed to cry. "Scarier guys than you." I couldn't help but add.

He jabbed the gun harder into my side making me shriek. "I don't think you should underestimate how scary I can be," he growled, and I was frightened. A Werewolf this close to the full moon was extremely dangerous.

He was leading me through the parking lot, he was no doubt about to shove me in his car. If I could get to my pepper spray when he let go of my arm, maybe I could risk running for it. "Didn't Logan tell you to stay out of town?"

"Logan isn't going to tell me to stay away from my wife and son."

"The wife you hit while she was pregnant with your son, why would you think they want to see you?"

"I don't give a shit what you think, Fawn. You're just an uppity Magician, you have no idea what I deal with as a Werewolf low on the totem. Everyone pushed me around all my life, that's nature, the strong command the weak. Well, I am not going to be weak anymore, I have something Logan wants and I plan to trade your ass for what *I* want."

"Logan isn't going to hand over an innocent Witch and infant to you. You're crazier than you look if you think this will work."

"Shut up!" He shoved me at an old beat-up Toyota. "Get in the driver's seat."

43

I took my opportunity, I grabbed my pepper spray and shot him right in the face. I couldn't believe my lucky aim. He dropped immediately and I ran to the one place I didn't think he would follow. Right to the nearest pier and jumped in. The water was frigid, but my adrenaline was pumping so I didn't hardly notice. I swam under a dock and hid behind a pilling. People were staring, they'd seen me jump in and he would know exactly where I was too if he came this way. It wasn't a perfect plan.

"A woman jumped in, call the police!" I heard someone say. Damn nosey humans. A red octopus swam near, drawing more attention from the humans above. "Look! An octopus!" I heard them start to shout, drawing a bigger crowd.

"Go," I shooed.

I swear it looked right into my eyes then jetted away, out into the open then began climbing a pilling on the pier across from me. The crowd of humans moved to watch, and I took the opportunity to slip in the other direction. If Kyle came down to the water, he would hopefully follow the crowd. I was probably safe for now if I was careful.

Fawn? A seal barked, slipping next to me in the water.

"Ummm, yes..." I answered, wondering how the hell this animal knew my name. Animals were usually simple creatures with very little use for words like names.

Sorry to confuse, it barked, *I am a Selkie, a friend of Eldoris. I have come to help.*

"Great, well you can start by showing me where I can climb out of this water unnoticed." The only things I knew about Selkies came from old storybooks, I had no idea they actually existed in the supernatural world, what the hell was going to find me next? I followed it for about a half mile then we came to an empty pier and I climbed out. The Selkie jumped out of the water smoothly, landing on the pier.

Then I witnessed one of the most disgusting things I had ever seen. The belly of the seal opened and out crawled a woman. Five feet tall, naked, and wet, silver hair and reflective silver eyes. "My name is Bay; I am here to represent the Selkies in this fight for our survival."

"Here put this on." I threw my rain jacket at her, we were going to look strange enough walking around soaking wet, if she were naked the cops would definitely be called. I pulled my phone out of my pocket, it was a total loss, completely soaked through and I had dropped my pepper spray too! "Damnit, I hope Betina is smart enough to wait at the car for me."

"Oh, a car! How exciting!" she squealed.

I couldn't help laughing, what was with these ocean supernaturals thinking cars were the coolest thing on land. "Watch out for an asshole with a gun, he's got short black hair and he was wearing a green jacket, his eyes will probably be red from the pepper spray still."

"Were you attacked! Are we in danger?" She looked around, worried. "Is it whoever is draining the ocean's power? Does he have Poseidon's stone?" She picked up the seal skin she had crawled out of and carefully folded it.

"Yes, I was attacked but no, I don't think we are in danger at the moment and not from whoever might have the stone. If we can get back to my house we will definitely be safe, its charmed to protect me."

"Neat, let's go." We started to walk swiftly. "So you have many enemies? I suppose that is a sign of a true protector of justice."

I liked her take on it. I couldn't protect justice without making a few enemies, I suppose I would just have to get used to *that*. We went directly to the car and gained many looks as we went. Mostly because we were soaking wet, at least it distracted from Bay's inhuman looks. Betina wasn't there waiting, and I was more than a little worried. What if Kyle had gone back and grabbed her! "I am not walking around wet, and you can't walk around in just a raincoat. I hope Betina found a ride home."

"Who's Betina?"

"A young Troll who lives with me, she was helping me investigate. I hope she didn't run into Kyle. If she isn't at the house, I'll be really worried."

"So do you have any leads?" Bay asked as we drove. She touched every button and stuck her hand out the window just like Eldoris had done.

"Only an idea, I'm hoping Betina had more luck than I did at the fish market."

"This is amazing!" she squealed when Journey's *Don't Stop Believing* blasted from the radio.

Chapter 5

When we got home, I rushed inside hoping to find Betina sitting on the couch. Evie was there and all the animals. Jake and Pete barked as Bay walked in behind me and the cats hurried over to meow about fish again.

"Another new friend!" Evie said, she was now dressed for the day in grey slacks and a purple blouse "who is this?"

"This is Bay, have you seen Betina?"

"Not since you two took off this morning. Why are you all wet?"

"Long story. Bay, I will get you something to wear, then I am going to shower. Where do you need to store *that*?" I said pointing to the pelt in her arms.

"Wherever your animals won't try and use it for a chew toy," she said, frowning at the cats.

"Go!" I told them and they scattered. "Sorry, they are intrigued by the new smell. You can put it in the cabinet over there." I pointed at the linen closet and went upstairs to grab something for her to wear. I wanted a hot shower and so much soap! Then I had to find Betina.

I handed Bay a sweater, underwear, and jeans. "Do you know how to put these on?"

Bay looked me up and down. "Like that?" she said pointing at me.

"Exactly."

"But what about these?" she asked holding up the red thong. "I don't see one of these on you."

"Oh, uh it goes on under the pants." I unzipped and flashed her the top of my own purple thong.

"Interesting, what is it for? It can't be for warmth."

"Its... uh, well I guess its to keep the pants from rubbing you the wrong way."

"You creatures are so odd," she laughed and dropped the raincoat in the middle of my living room. Evie screeched and disappeared.

I hurried away; she would just have to figure it out on her own. I stripped quickly and stepped under the hottest water I could stand, letting it thaw me completely. Then I grabbed the soap and started to scrub. When I was just starting to feel clean again my bathroom door flew open and I nearly jumped out of my skin.

"Are you alive, Fawn?" Annabel called from the doorway.

"Christ, Annabel you scared the crap out of me, what the hell are you doing?" Annabel was a Witch half Elf who had become a good friend of mine and had helped solve the last mystery I'd been investigating. She lived in what I would describe as a wild sorority house of Witches that were even crazier than her and apparently didn't believe in privacy.

"Logan called nearly biting my head off through the phone because he can't get ahold of you and Betina told him you disappeared at the market."

"I had a little mishap and needed a shower, is Betina okay?"

"Yeah, I picked her up downtown and brought her home. I met Bay downstairs, helped her figure out how to put on a thong... she said you were in the sound."

I turned off the water and got out of the shower. "Yeah, that was part of the mishap. So call Logan, tell him I'm alive."

"Betina is a little pissed at you and I am *not* calling Logan, you call him."

"My phone is destroyed." Annabel threw hers at me, her bright purple eyes flashing. "Thanks," I grumbled.

"You're welcome, I will go downstairs and pretend I don't know you're getting yelled at," she smiled. Her short black hair was flipped up at the bottom today and sleeked back behind her pointy ears. She was wearing a black dress with a purple corset over top and heeled black boots with lots of buckles. She looked like a perfect dark princess, though if I said that she would get super pissed at me, she didn't like people thinking she was delicate in any way.

"You're very kind," I said sarcastically as she left. I dialed Logan, not sure what I was going to tell him. I didn't want to interrupt his full moon ceremony and I also didn't want to act like I couldn't take care of myself.

"Annabel, what happened to Fawn?" Logan's frantic voice answered the phone after the first ring.

"I'm fine, Logan."

"Fawn! Why weren't you answering your phone and why the hell did you leave Betina at the market?"

"Its not a big deal, and I don't want you to leave Brakemoor."

"What is it?" Logan growled.

"Betina and I went to the market to see if anything was amiss, I had this epiphany that a human might want the stone to harness the ocean power for fishing. Catch the biggest, the best, and make money."

"Yes," he growled.

"So we went down to ask around and look around and... promise you aren't going to freak out."

"I can't do that, Fawn. I am hours from the full moon and about to crush this phone in my hand, what happened?"

"Well, I was at the market and Kyle found me."

"Kyle!" His voice exploded and I had to hold the phone away from my ear. "That bastard Werewolf shouldn't be anywhere near Seattle!"

"Well, he wanted to trade me for his wife and son apparently. But I got away easy enough, jumped in the sound and met Bay, a Selkie." Silence met my words and I thought for a moment that Logan had crushed the phone, but then I heard a growl and I knew, he had shifted. "Logan!" I yelled. "Everything is fine, I will see you tomorrow."

No! Logan growled but I hung up the phone, no use trying to calm him down now. Hopefully, his pack could reason with him. He wasn't likely to lope back here in wolf form anyway, I hoped.

I got dressed in jeans and a sweatshirt then went downstairs. Betina, Annabel, Eldoris, Bay, and Evie were sitting around the living room. Chester landed on my shoulder as I came into the room tweeting *hello*. Pete and Jake were sleeping by the front door, good guard dogs that they were and the cats were sniffing Eldoris and Bay, confused. *Fish*, they meowed off and on. "My cats are intrigued by your scents."

"Yes, they are quite the interesting creatures," Bay said.

"What the hell happened to you?" Betina demanded. "I turned around and you were gone! I searched everywhere and the cute fish guy thought I was nuts, thank you."

"I was almost taken hostage by an angry, abusive Werewolf."

"What!" They all gasped at once, even Bay who had already heard the story.

"Yeah, Kyle," I said looking at Annabel.

"Shit, I better warn Tara," Annabel said. I handed her back her phone and she stepped outside to call.

51

"What's with Kyle and Tara?" Betina asked.

"Kyle is a Werewolf, Tara is a Witch, his wife, and they had a child recently. Kyle was abusive though, so Logan kicked him out of town and Tara moved back in with the Witches. Only now Kyle seems to want his family back and was going to hold me hostage for trade I guess."

"Oh my! Are you okay?" Evie gasped.

"Yeah, I maced him and jumped in the sound, which is where I met Bay, and destroyed my phone. Did you find out anything at the fish market, Betina?"

"No, I almost had his number but I noticed you were out of sight, and I had to go look for you," she whined.

"We should stake out the docks when the boats go out again, I still don't think we are wrong in our assumption."

"Great so that's what, like two am?" Betina groaned.

"Well on the plus side that gives us plenty of time to replace my phone and pepper spray."

"Maybe you need a stun gun," Annabel added, coming back inside.

I bit my lip; I really didn't like violence.

It was easier to buy mace and a stun gun than replace a broken cell phone! Cheaper too. Humans were backwards, which is why we didn't trust them to know about supernaturals. But I managed to do it all, with an entourage that included a half Elf half Witch, a Troll, a Selkie and an Octopus Shifter. We did not get it done without quite a few curious looks though. Especially when we were in the cell phone store and the two little ocean creatures couldn't stop cooing and laughing over the thing called a cell phone they'd heard so much about. I think people started to assume they were from some cult, just barely let out of the barn.

I even managed to get to the studio in time to teach a couple classes. Tonight was slow, no Werewolves, so I had offered a special class for the Witches and they came in droves. With Annabel's help, we incanted a fire in the middle of the room, a shower of lavender and chamomile scent from the ceiling, and the quiet sounds of a gentle river from the speakers which was also visible in the mirror. It was amazing and I was certain to repeat the themed night again, maybe every full moon.

"That was so wonderful, Fawn," Misty, the leader of the local Witch coven and Annabel's mother, said as she rolled her yoga mat. "I heard what happened between you and Kyle," she frowned.

"Yeah, don't worry, Logan will take care of him." I just hoped he would take care of him before he found his way to Tara and the child.

"We can protect our own. You be careful." She walked out then, and I was left wondering why she'd bothered mentioning it at all. She wasn't going to offer me any protection or thank me for trying to protect one of hers! Witches...

Chapter 6

Two hours before sunrise our group was sneaking around the shadows of the Seattle fishing docks. We were all dressed like cat burglars, and I must say, we looked good.

"What exactly are we looking for?" Betina asked.

"Other than an obvious show of the stone?" I sighed. "Anything out of the ordinary."

"Right, because I definitely know what is ordinary about this whole damn fishing situation," Betina grumbled.

"Eldoris and Bay, why don't you slip into the water and swim around, maybe you can sense the stone."

"Okay," they said, and both began to undress quickly. Bay laid out her seal skin and slipped inside, the skin sealed itself and she slid into the water, I almost couldn't believe what I saw. Then Eldoris jumped and midair shifted into a red octopus and hit the water with a small splash. I recognized that octopus! She'd been in the sound with me yesterday, she'd helped pull the human's attention away from me!

"Badass!" Betina said.

"Annabel, can you cloak yourself well enough to walk around the men without notice?"

"No problem," she said and slipped away mumbling a spell.

"Now we wait and watch from here I think," I told Betina, and we both stayed close in the shadow, watching men move around the docks and boats. "I didn't love taking such a passive role in the investigation, but I didn't have any kind of cloaking ability and neither did Betina.

"Do you think Logan would approve of this?"

"Definitely not, but maybe we don't mention it."

"You want me to lie to him!" Betina acted shocked and I punched her playfully. "You know I am only loyal to you," she said with a serious tone.

I believed it too, she was only here, above ground because of me. Living a life that included work and dating and fun. Of course, I was happy to do it, she had turned out to be a real wonderful part of my life.

"What are you lovely ladies up to this time of night, in a place like this?"

Betina and I both jumped at the voice, we spun around and I pulled out my stun gun. When I bought it, I wasn't sure if I would be able to use it, but standing there in the dark I did it without a second thought. I would do whatever necessary to protect Betina and myself. As the buzz lit up the shadow so did the smell of rotten milk and fish, Betina was defending us as well. The man shook, groaned, and hit the ground hard.

We both stared, unmoving for a full minute. The man didn't move either. We leaned close. "That's no human," Betina said.

"I can't even think right now," I said. "Can you tone down your magical stench?" When I could concentrate again, I had to agree, this was no human. "A Vampire?"

"Maybe he's just pale because you shocked the crap out of him," Betina suggested.

"Take a closer look, if he was human, I might have killed him."

"You take a closer look!" Betina whispered harshly.

I held the stun gun ready and leaned closer to the body. "He's not breathing."

"Dead not breathing, or Vampire not breathing?" She asked.

"How am I supposed to know?" I whispered a little too harshly, this was *not* part of the plan. In fact, this was exactly why I didn't want to carry weapons. If I start killing humans I'm going to end up in my father's basement behind bars.

"Feel for a pulse, Vampires have a pulse, don't they?"

I knew enough about Vampire anatomy to know that was true, they didn't have to breathe but their blood pumped through their body, full of oxygen

57

from the blood they drank from humans. "Okay, take the stun gun. If he moves, shock him again." I handed Betina the stun gun and she moved to stand on the other side of the body. She held the stun gun close to his stomach, ready. He was dressed in black slacks and t-shirt, boots and a leather jacket, goth enough to be a Vampire. The clothes looked a little out of date, but not enough to be overly obvious, Vampires didn't tend to dress with the times, but more in a timeless fashion. I was starting to feel hopeful, shocking a Vampire into unconsciousness wasn't a crime. "Okay, here I go..." I reached down and pressed two fingers to the side of his throat and waited. "Yes!" I said, a little too loud apparently because Betina got spooked and shocked the poor Vampire again. The smell of rotten milk and fish was again assaulting my nose and burning my eyes.

"Uh-oh, well if he wasn't dead before, he might be now." She dropped the stun gun and stepped back.

I stepped away too, mostly from the smell Betina was emitting. I wasn't afraid of the stunned Vampire at this point. "He's a Vampire, the shock won't kill him, but I don't know how long he'll be out, we can't leave him here where the sun could get to him." If I were in any way responsible for a Vampire's untimely death, that would mean serious trouble with Cassius Vamprose, the leader of the U.S. Vampires and a very scary being.

"And what do you suggest we do, drag him to the car and shove him in the trunk?" Betina said. I looked at her and shrugged, I didn't have a better idea. She sighed, "I'll grab his legs, I don't want to be anywhere near that mouth when he wakes up." I grabbed under his armpits and Betina lifted his legs then we shuffled back to where we had parked Annabel's car. "You know, he's kind of cute."

"In an almost dead I want to rip out your throat and suck you dry kind of way?" I said sarcastically.

"Exactly!"

We dropped his body in the trunk and I slammed the lid. I stepped back slowly, half expecting it to burst open and the Vampire to come out in a rage.

"What if hottie Vampire wakes up in there?" Betina asked.

"Well... hopefully we aren't in the car when he does. He can just bust out and walk away, that would be great." I didn't add what I was really thinking, which was hopefully he'd leave without figuring out who we were or trying to get any kind of revenge for the harsh treatment. I didn't need the Vampire community thinking I was prejudice or afraid of them, though I was.

"What if he's friends with Drake or Zin and they bring him to the house one day and he's like oh my god you tazed me and locked me in a trunk."

I looked at Betina like she had lost it, because in what world would something like that happen. "Let's go back to watch the docks."

"It could happen," she mumbled.

We hurried back to our position then moved closer, sticking to shadows that wouldn't have really hidden us if anyone cared to look. Men were loading things onto boats and shouting to each other about how they were going to out fish the other.

"No one can beat Jeff lately!" one shouted.

"Ha! Beginner's luck is all that is!" someone shouted back.

"Sounds like Jeff might be who we're looking for," I whispered.

"Ya, but which one's Jeff?"

"I guess whoever comes back with the biggest haul. Early fish market for restaurants is at six, we'll be first in line."

The boats left soon after that with no further clue as to who Jeff might be. Annabel slinked back with a smile.

"Did you find anything?" I asked hopefully.

"There's a newer boat, its green. The guys on it were real quiet loading and getting ready and they didn't hurry out, they were the last to leave the dock. If I had to bet, that is our guy."

"Jeff?" I asked.

"No one actually addressed him, so I can't say for sure, but yeah I heard the talk too. Seems like Jeff might be our guy and I'm betting Jeff has the newer green boat."

Bay and Eldoris slipped out of the water. Bay unzipped and folded her skin neatly. Eldoris emerged fully reformed into a human.

"Did you ladies see anything?" I asked as they got dressed.

"I could definitely sense the stone, its on one of those boats," Bay said.

"Yes, I could as well," Eldoris agreed. "It seemed strongest around the green boat."

"Green boat, good. We are pretty sure we are looking for someone named Jeff," I said, feeling confident now. Everyone's investigations meshed.

"Jeff on a green boat, that should be simple enough to find at the early market," Betina said. "Now what about the Vampire in Annabel's trunk?

Bay and Eldoris looked at me with more than a little shock. "A what in your what?" Bay said.

"What did you do!" Annabel gritted out between clenched teeth.

"Yeah, well, we were attacked!" Betina defended.

"More like surprised," I admitted. "We may have hurried to use the stun gun; I knew it was a bad idea to get me a weapon. He passed out and I didn't want him to wake up in the sun here or get in the way of our stakeout, so we put him in the trunk for safe keeping."

Annabel laughed and I glared at her. "Makes sense," she said.

"Well, it's at least an hour until sunrise, don't you think its safe to let him out?" Bay said.

"Unless he's awake and angry, yeah I suppose so," I said nervously.

"He's super cute too," Betina said.

"Maybe Bay and I should open the trunk, Vampires don't like our blood," Eldoris suggested.

"Thanks, but I think I should, I wouldn't want anyone else to get hurt because of me." The last thing I wanted was for this unfortunate mishap to hurt anyone else. We walked to the car; it looked the same as we had left it. The girls spread out around the trunk, keeping a bit of distance. I was thankful for their support. I handed the stun gun to Betina again. "Only if *absolutely* necessary," I said with a frown.

"Sure," she said with a smile. "Wouldn't want to hurt hottie the Vampire." She winked and I rolled my eyes.

I opened the trunk and jumped back. We all gasped; it was empty. "What the hell?" I put my hands on my hips and stared into the trunk. It was exactly what I had hoped would happen, he woke up and left, without killing us. So why was I disappointed?

"Not that being kidnapped by five beautiful women isn't appealing, I just am not sure I could survive your idea of foreplay."

We all swung around at the words and there stood the Vampire we had stuck in the trunk. His dark blue eyes stared at me, piercing, they looked like an ocean during a storm and I had a feeling his soul matched.

"But maybe I would try," he said with a raised eyebrow and a rakish grin. His eyes looked me up and down with a slow sensual glide. "What's your name, love?"

"Fawn," I said, a little shakily, then took a steadying breath and put my hands on my hips. "Sneaking up on women in the dark is not a good way to make friends," I said a little angrily.

He smiled and I had to admit his face was pleasant to look at, for a Vampire. "Unintentional, I promise. I can't help if I am naturally quiet in my movements. I was only interested in why a Troll and a beautiful Magician would be standing in shadow, watching a bunch of human men loading fishing boats before sunrise. Now I wonder why a Witch, a Selkie and a Shifter are part of your odd pack. You *are* their leader I assume." He looked at me and raised an eyebrow.

Somehow, I felt like he was complimenting me and I liked it. A rush of pride ran through me. "I am, as far as you are concerned."

"You have a certain air about you," he continued. "I find women in charge to be quite attractive, I must admit." He stepped closer; his eyes boring into mine with an intensity that I wasn't sure I wanted to be close to. "There's something sexy about dominance in such a small fragile frame," he whispered.

I took a step back and felt my mistake immediately in the way his grin turned predatory. I stood up straighter to try and make up for it. "Are you okay? We didn't intend to harm you, only to keep you from waking up in the sun." I didn't want him to think we didn't care that we'd possibly hurt him, but I got the feeling that wasn't on his mind now anyway.

"I appreciate your concern after shocking me unconscious." His voice was heavy with sarcasm but still somehow light. "I am fine, however still curious. I don't find too many things that pique my curiosity these days."

I had a feeling he was talking about more than just why we were all out here and I didn't like the curiosity it was conjuring up in my own mind. I caught myself staring at the way his lips curled up and as I watched, his tongue darted out swiftly, tantalizing. My face heated, knowing he'd done it because I was staring, as if he could read my lecherous thoughts. I shook myself internally. More like his lecherous thoughts projected into my mind! This was *not* me!

"We are investigating official business," Betina said snarkily. "*This* is Fawn Malero, ever heard of her?" No one could turn the table quite like a teen. I could feel my pack of females moving closer together, supporting me as their leader. I just hoped none of them noticed my lapse in judgement.

The Vampire smiled brightly. "In fact I have! I believe you are quite close with my brother, Drake. I am Dante."

"Drake's brother! Oh my, it's so nice to meet you, Dante," I said quickly, I did *not* want to piss off a member of the Vamprose family.

"And you, Fawn," he said familiarly, "And since you have detained me so close to sunrise, can I trouble you for a place to spend the day? I just arrived in town and haven't had a chance to secure a room unfortunately."

Him in my house was the last thing I wanted. "Of course!" I said between gritted teeth. I didn't have a reason to deny him a safe place from the sun. "Do you have a vehicle nearby?"

"No, I'll hop in with you ladies, if that's alright."

Again, there was nothing I could do but agree. "Of course," I said grudgingly.

We all piled into the car. It was an awkwardly silent ride home. I stared at the back of Dante's head as Annabel drove. There was a familiarity to his face I now recognized as being similar to Drake who I had come to trust wholeheartedly. But I still didn't feel overly comfortable with all Vampires. Their feeding habits disturbed me, both as a vegetarian and as a potential victim. Why was he here, I wondered? Why wasn't he staying with Drake? Or even my father would have happily offered a room in his basement. He was often obligated to offer lodging to supernaturals passing through town since he was in charge of this area. Things definitely didn't add up with Dante, why was he on foot and why hadn't Drake mentioned his brother was coming to town? What had he been doing down by the docks? That was easy, he was probably looking for an easy meal when he stumbled onto us expecting prostitutes. Why did looking at him make my heart speed, my breath quicken and my knees weak! I shook my head; those were not the questions to concentrate on right now.

I was so deep in my wondering that when he finally broke the silence I jumped, then Eldoris squealed. "I would appreciate if you asked Drake to come to the house at sunset, I have an important message to deliver," he said, turning slightly and grinning at my jumpiness. "Do you always tremble so, at the sound of a man's voice?" he teased.

I glared at him, not caring that I might be pissing off a Vamprose at this point. "Why can't you tell him?" I asked suspicious. Did Drake even know his brother was in town? Would Drake even *want* to see his brother?

"He isn't inclined to answer my messages on a regular basis," he said with a bitter laugh.

"And why is that?" Betina pressed tactlessly.

Dante smiled at us, it was a very nice smile, he had bright white teeth and dimples! A Vampire with dimples, that was interesting. "Ah, family drama, I don't think I care to share such personal information, at least until we get to know each other better."

The last words were meant for me and they were full of innuendo. I bit my lip as images popped into my head unwelcome. What the hell was wrong with me? Maybe the full moon was affecting my libido just as much as it affected the Werewolf's.

"Drake will tell me," Betina said confidently.

Dante looked at her curiously. "And who are you to my *sweet* brother?"

The way he said sweet made me think he didn't find the trait worthy. There was definitely something between the two brothers and I was not sure I wanted to be in the middle.

"Only like his best friend," Betina scoffed.

"Well, nice to meet you then."

"Betina," Betina said.

"Nice to meet you, Betina."

I bit my lip realizing I hadn't made any introductions, I was forgetting all my manners, and my boyfriend! Looking at this intriguing Vampire. "Betina has recently come under my care. This is

Eldoris and Bay, they are staying with me for a while and Annabel."

"Do you run a boarding house?" He asked quite seriously.

"Well, *I* don't live with her," Annabel said. "I just come over to go on adventures now and again," Annabel laughed. "But yes, she does seem to take in the weak and weary often enough."

I laughed, that was a rather good description. "I suppose I'll have to have Logan's crew add some more rooms in the back."

"Logan Licard?" Dante asked without emotion, but it set off my radar immediately.

"Yes," I said with an equal amount of no inflection. Of course, Betina didn't read the car well.

"They are like totally in love, it's disgusting," Betina said, and I was surprised she didn't make a gag motion to go with it.

Something ran across Dante's blue eyes and they widened just the slightest, but he turned around quickly so I couldn't see more. "Interesting," he said quietly.

When we arrived back at the house everyone breathed a sigh of relief to get out of the car. We walked into the house and Evie met us with wide eyes and a huge grin. Pete and Jake watched curiously and Chester tweeted a happy greeting from a top shelf.

"Who is this handsome devil?" Evie asked.

"This is Dante, Drake's brother," I said.

"Dante! Welcome to our home," Evie said grandly, waving her arm.

"I can show you to the basement," I said, in a hurry to get some space from him.

Friend, friend! Friend? Pumpkin meowed coming into the room and sniffing Dante. He bent and patted her quickly which surprised me. I guess I would have thought he'd have more likely kicked her away or bitten her.

"Pumpkin is your brother's biggest fan," I said. "She thinks you might be the same person."

"My brother and a pet cat, interesting," he said with the same flat tone he'd used in the car. I really didn't trust him. He had gone from overtly sexual innuendos to not expressing a thing. Whatever he was hiding couldn't be good for me.

"They became attached when I was nursing his wounds here," I explained, then regretted it. Why was I giving him more information!

"Wounds?" he asked quickly, his eyes widening slightly. "Are you a nurse of some kind?"

I knew nothing about this man, I wasn't even positive he was who he said he was. Even if he did look a bit like Drake, and Pumpkin thought they smelled quite similar. "Yeah, something like that, I'm sure Drake will tell you all about it."

"Right, make sure you message him to be here after sunset," he said with a touch of force that I didn't appreciate.

"I certainly will," I assured him as I showed him down into the basement. And I would, I wanted this mystery solved sooner rather than later. "Do you need anything? I will be in and out all day."

"With your secret fishing mission?" he said with a smile and closed the distance between us.

Suddenly I found myself close enough to this mystery Vampire to feel his breath on my face and the heat from his body was washing over me. I could feel my own body heat up in response and my breathing became labored. I swallowed, trying to center myself. It didn't work. "Exactly," I stammered.

"I should be quite comfortable here, though lonely," he said with one raised eyebrow and he grinned wide enough to show those enticing dimples.

I swallowed hard as images infected my mind again; our bodies twisted and sweating, touching. I coughed, choking on my own desire. "I-I will see you at sunset."

He sighed as if resigning himself to my refusal. "I don't suppose you have a blood supply?"

"Sorry, no." I said taking a step back, thankful for some space so I could gather my thoughts correctly.

He laughed at my obvious discomfort. "Don't worry, Fawn. I have no interest in your blood, though I am sure it would be as sweet as your disposition."

"Thanks..." I said, not comforted. I had a very good idea of what he *was* interested in. "I will see you this evening." I hurried away and sighed heavily when the basement door shut between us. I was tempted to lock it but didn't think that would be a good idea. I'd already locked him in a trunk tonight, and that hadn't held him anyway. There was something about him that scrambled my brain! I had never in my life been attracted to a Vampire and here I was nearly drooling over this one I'd just met. Something didn't make sense.

"What do you think his deal is?" Annabel asked, coming into the kitchen. The other girls were sitting in the living room giggling as they watched some reality dating show.

"I don't know, but I don't trust him."

"He's kinda cute." Annabel waited but when I didn't respond she went on. "Are you going to message Drake?"

"Definitely, I need to know if he is who he says he is and if he's safe to be around. Of course, Drake probably won't check it until sunset." I already knew the answer to the question of safety, he was definitely not safe to be around, at least not for me. I pulled out my phone and texted: *Have a Vampire in my basement, says he's your brother, Dante...*

"Are you going to message Logan?" Annabel asked when I set my phone down.

That was harder. I looked at the closed door. Jake and Pete were sitting and staring at the door, like they did when Drake had been down there. I had been wrong about Drake when we first met, he turned out to be a wonderfully nice man, even for a Vampire. I had been wrong about Xander too, he had turned out to be a liar and a killer, even though he was a Warlock. I didn't dare fully trust my own judgement where Dante was concerned. "I don't think so, at least not until I hear back from Drake.

70

Logan will be back here before sundown anyway." I didn't want to talk to Logan until I had settled these feelings anyway. "It's a few hours until we have to be back at the docks, I am going to try and get a few minutes of sleep," I grumbled, sure it wouldn't happen.

Annabel left but would be back to pick us up. I slipped upstairs to rest, and the three giggling girls looked like they were perfectly happy to watch tv with Evie. I slipped into bed fully clothed and set my mace and stun gun on the nightstand, just in case. At least I knew I could incapacitate a Vampire with the stun gun, which was handy. I drifted to sleep with too many questions running around my head. My dreams were strange, full of dark corners promising earthly delights and a wave of dark seawater crashing through walls, filling up, drowning me. Then a strong arm, I grasped it expecting Logan, I turned and saw Dante's face grinning sensually, his fangs dripping with blood. I tried to scream but his mouth crushed mine and I was floating on a wave of pleasure so intense I was shaking and moaning...

Chapter 7

"Fawn! Wake up!"

I bolted up in bed, my heart racing and looked around the room confused. Thankfully, no Dante. There was a lot of sunlight pouring in, what time was it? "Annabel?"

"Yeah, everyone is asleep, and we need to get to the docks if we have any hope of seeing what Jeff brings in. Sorry to interrupt what sounded like a *very* pleasant dream." Her eyes were suspicious, and I had a feeling she knew it wasn't Logan's kiss I'd been enjoying in that dream.

I ignored the last comment. "Shit, okay." I rubbed my eyes and grabbed the pepper spray, no need for the stun gun on this mission. I was still dressed like a cat burglar and thought it might be a little too obvious, so I traded my black sweater for a bright pink one and threw on a beanie. "We can let the others sleep; we'll probably be less obvious if its just us anyway."

"Before I woke you up it uh... sounded like you were saying Dante..." She wasn't going to let it go.

"It was a nightmare," I said quickly and headed out the door.

"Alright, let's go."

"You're up early," Evie said as we snuck downstairs. The dogs were sleeping by the basement door and the cats were nowhere to be found, probably sleeping off their nocturnal activities. Chester gave me a good morning tweet and I got a little birdseed out for him.

"Yes, fish markets open early," I explained.

"I thought you were one of those vegetarians," Evie said with a little condescension.

"I am, we are looking for someone who is using a magical amulet from Poseidon to take power from the ocean and catch more fish than humanly possible," I said matter of factly.

Evie just threw up her hands and huffed, "You young'uns and your weird diets, in my day we ate whatever was cheap and nutritious."

"Okay, Evie," I laughed. "We will be back soon, if the girls wake up let them know we went ahead without them."

"Will do," she said happily.

"Its quite handy to have Evie here, she never leaves so she's dependable for message delivery," I said as we got into Annabel's car.

"Speaking of messages, did we hear from Drake?"

"Oh! Damn I left my phone upstairs."

"You seem a little distracted, is it because of your... nightmare?"

"Well, you were rushing me," I complained.

"Yeah, and we still might be too late. The boats head back out for another round of morning fishing after they unload for the early market. If we don't find Jeff this morning we will have to wait until noon."

I frowned; I didn't have a plan. What were we going to do when we did identify the guy? Just because we know who he is doesn't mean we've solved the problem.

Annabel was thinking the same thing. "What are we going to do when we identify Jeff?"

"I have no idea, honestly. We need to be sure that he has the stone, do you think you'll be able to sense its magic if we get close enough?"

"I might, my Elf side is tuned in with old magic like the stone has."

"Then we need to get close," I said, determined to handle this. We parked near the early fish market and it was already bustling. "We should pick up some shellfish for Bay and Eldoris while we're here."

"If there is anything left," Annabel said doubtfully as we walked toward the market. There were dozens of people buying up boxes and boxes of seafood for their restaurants.

We walked until we found the green boat and a man set up in front of it with his catch. "That must be Jeff," I said.

The man was young, no more than thirty I would guess. Blonde hair, long enough to stick out from under his beanie and green eyes. He was tall and athletic looking, not bulging with muscles but definitely capable of lots of physical activity. It wouldn't be easy to rip a magical stone away from him if he wasn't willing to give it up. We walked forward slowly, as if we were just checking things out. We stopped at his booth and perused, semi-interested.

"What can I help you lovely ladies with today?" He asked coming over.

"Hi, I'm Fawn," I said holding out my hand to force an introduction.

"I'm Jeff and I own this fishing outfit here, what are you interested in?"

"Other than you," Annabel said coming forward with a seductive smile and holding out her hand. "I'm Annabel."

He turned to her and shook her hand. "Nice to meet you, Annabel," he said, smiling warmly.

"We are interested in what you do here, do you give private tours of your vessel," she asked, heavy on the innuendo.

I wasn't sure this was going to work; he would probably think we were prostitutes at this point. If we had been relying on my flirting abilities, I guarantee that's what he'd be thinking. Annabel was smoother, maybe he would buy it.

His eyes narrowed a bit, not buying it. "A tour huh, not interested in purchasing fish today?"

I stepped forward, ready to try another tactic. "Actually, we are more interested in a fishing adventure. Do you do that?"

"I don't, sorry ladies."

I heard Annabel mumble something behind me and smelled some herb, then she stepped forward and touched Jeff's arm. "Take us on a tour," she said quietly.

He looked at her with a sort of blank face. "Why don't I show you two the boat," he said mechanically.

"Good move," I whispered.

"I could feel him closing off to us, he wasn't buying our story at all," she responded. "He might have thought we were trying to trick him into a prostitution situation."

I couldn't help laughing, humans had simple minds to predict. We followed him to the boat, there were more than a few curious looks from his crew, but no one said anything. Once we stepped onto the boat, Annabel touched him again.

"Show us your secret to catching so many fish," she said quietly. He spun on his heels and started walking toward the stairs. We descended into a small galley, and he continued back to a living space. He reached under the mattress and pulled out a small wooden box.

I gasped and reached out for it, but it must have been too much because his grip tightened, and his eyes blinked. "What the hell!" he said.

"Damn," Annabel said harshly.

"We need this," I said, not letting go either. We stared at each other; I was no match for him physically, even with Annabel to back me up we would probably lose a fair fight. "It doesn't belong to you, you have no idea what it's magic is costing," I pleaded. Maybe I could get him to see, to agree that humans shouldn't be messing with this sort of thing.

"I bought it, its mine and *I* need it," he spat.

Predictably dense and selfish human. "It's *not* yours, it belongs to the ocean."

"No bitch is going to take it from me." He pushed the box toward me making me lose my footing, I had to let go as I fell back, knocking Annabel over too. Jeff took the opportunity to catapult himself over us in the small galley and started up the stairs as we scrambled to our feet.

Annabel whispered and made a movement with her hand, his feet collapsed under him and he fell back down the stairs. I didn't even think, I pulled out the pepper spray and shot him. He screamed and unfortunately so did we, the small space swirled the spray into our eyes too. "Fuck!" I yelled grabbing blindly for the box.

"What the hell is going on down there?" A voice called from above deck. "Jeff?"

"Annabel, cloak us!" I yelled, still searching for the box. Jeff was scrambling too, apparently having dropped it.

Annabel mumbled just as the man appeared at the entrance to the stairs.

"Jeff, you down there? What the hell is that smell?"

"Frank! Call the police, these bitches are trying to steal from me!"

78

"He can't hear you," Annabel hissed. "Where's the god damn box!"

We were all on hands and knees bumping around the small space, frantic. Jeff took a leap for the stairs, and I knew he must have found it. I leaped too, catching him around the neck and forcing all my weight to pull him back down. I landed hard on my back with Jeff on top of me, his elbow caught me in the ribs and I let my grip go with a groan. Annabel was right there shoving something into his face and he collapsed.

"Fawn, are you alright?"

"I can't breathe," I groaned, still under him.

Annabel pulled him off of me and grabbed the box, "Let's go, he'll be awake again in a minute."

Still not really able to see straight, we hurried up the stairs, shoving past Frank who looked very confused. We must have appeared out of thin air to him.

"What the hell? Jeff!" he yelled down the stairwell again. "What's going on?"

We didn't stop running until we reached the safety of Annabel's car. We were breathing heavy, and our eyes were red and watering, but we were successful! Annabel handed me the box.

"I hope this is it, because I don't think we can show our faces down there again without getting arrested," I panted.

"It is, I can feel it," she panted back.

It was a very simple wooden box with a brass latch. I opened it slowly and gasped. The stone looked like it was made from pure water. It seemed to swirl and shimmer. "This is definitely it." I picked up the stone gently and the magic it held was unmistakable. It washed through me like lightning, and I dropped it back in the box. "So much power! How had a human even stood to touch it?"

"Humans don't feel the magic like we do, to them it would feel like a dull pulse if anything."

"I feel like I was minorly electrocuted." But somehow in a good way, it was hard to explain.

"I wish we had been able to ask Jeff some questions, like where the hell he got it!" Annabel said, looking at the stone with an amazed smile.

I poked around the box for a clue, careful not to touch the stone itself more than I had to. I was not surprised to find a simple white card with a silver S on it. I held it up and frowned. "Mr. S is a real problem."

"Stefan did this you think?"

"Definitely, this card is just like the one Stefan gave me when we met. He really should be more subtle. Of course, that's not a Magicians strength." It was going to be that Magician's undoing. It wasn't a simple misjudgment, he was continually selling things to humans that could not only reveal the supernatural community, but it could also harm them.

"What do we do with the stone?" Annabel asked, starting the car and putting some needed distance between us and Jeff."

"It needs to be returned to the ocean, I'm just not sure who should be in charge of getting it where it needs to be."

"Maybe before we tell everyone we found it, we should know who needs to receive it," Annabel suggested.

"And how do we figure that one out?" I asked a little frustrated that we didn't have a plan.

"Maybe your father knows where it came from in the first place?"

I groaned, I didn't really want to involve my father, I would rather just tell him after it was over that I had solved it. Annabel was right though, we needed to know where it was going before we told anyone we had it. I sent Betina a message with Annabel's phone reminding her to get to the studio to teach her classes and suggesting she might take the girls with her. I didn't want anyone venturing downstairs while Dante was down there.

We pulled up to my parent's house a few minutes later and carried the box inside. I kept the card in my pocket, I wasn't ready to reveal that tidbit yet.

"Fawn! Annabel, how wonderful to see you two," my mother said as Julie, our devoted maid, led us into the living room. Julie had been with my family since I could remember. She was a Magician, but no abilities had ever developed in her and my parents had taken her into their home, given her a place to live and work as long as she wanted to. She'd never left, and she seemed happy with her place.

"Can I get you girls some refreshments?" Julie asked.

"No, thank you Julie. Hello mother, father." I gave them quick hugs.

"To what do we owe the pleasure of our only daughter's company?" my father said with a raised brow. I hadn't visited since I was here to see Xander locked up in the basement, it wasn't a pleasant memory.

"What do you know about Poseidon's stone?" I asked as Annabel and I took a seat.

"Oh!" my mother gasped.

"It's been lost for centuries, but it is very powerful," my father said carefully. "Could be used to drain all of the power of the ocean and harness it for whatever the keeper wants."

"And before it was lost, where was it? Who had it?" I pressed.

My father looked at us curiously then down at the box in my lap. "Is that it?"

"Maybe..."

He smiled approvingly. "It belongs to every supernatural creature in the ocean, Poseidon left it to his four daughters. One was a Selkie, one was a Shifter, one was a Mermaid, and one was a Siren. They guarded it in a cave in the deepest part of the ocean. Legend says there was born a Siren who fell in love with an Elf, but she couldn't leave the ocean for more than a day without returning to regain the power that the stone bestowed on them all. So she stole it, brought it on land so she could live with her love. Since that day, the creatures of the ocean have not trusted any who walk on land."

"But Eldoris said that Fanlin was the one who told her to find me for help," I interrupted, confused.

"Well, I suppose there would be some friendliness between the Water Elf clan that lives out on the peninsula and the ocean creatures, they are said to be descendents of the couple who ran off together. They are particularly drawn to the ocean but have no abilities to live in it," he said thoughtfully. "I never took too much stock in the legend, but maybe."

"That doesn't really help though, who would it be returned to, if found?" I asked.

My father chuckled at my unwillingness to admit it was sitting right here in the box. "It should be returned to the sea; you would need to find a representative from each of the four clans willing to take on the responsibility of its protection I suppose."

"Great, like a Selkie and Octopus Shifter aren't enough, now I need a Mermaid and a Siren! My house is definitely not that big."

"What about that Elf clan? Shouldn't they have a representation too then? They seem like they are a part of it as well," Annabel said thoughtfully.

"I suppose..." my father said cocking his head to the side. "Of course, *you*, could make that decision, couldn't you, Annabel? Your father, I believe was of that clan."

Annabel frowned. "My mother won't say for sure, but," she looked at the box. "I certainly feel a connection to the stone."

"It might be best to think about that before going forward. May I see it?" he asked, and I was filled with pride knowing he was respecting my possession of the jewel and jurisdiction over the case as a whole. I opened the box and my parents crowded around to ooh and ahh at it.

"What's all this?"

I slammed the box shut and we all turned to the voice. My brother, Chase had walked into the room.

"Woah, interrupting something good I see," Chase said coming forward.

"Nothing of importance to you, Chase," I said holding the box close.

"Well, I suppose if you don't want to tell me, I will just have to wait and drag the information out of Betina," he said with a wink.

I glared, knowing he probably would be able to do just that. However, I wasn't planning on telling Betina just yet.

"I will let you know what we decide," I said to my father and gave my parents quick kisses before leaving.

"Hey, Fawn!" Chase called, following us to the door. "Betina said you were attacked by a Werewolf?" he whispered, concerned.

"Yeah, but it wasn't a big deal."

"Does this have to do with Cole?"

"No, its something else. Don't worry, I'm having really good luck with pepper spray as protection," I said with a wink.

"And Logan?"

"Yeah, he'll be back today. Hey, do you know anything about Dante Vamprose?"

"As in Drake's brother? No, sorry. Why?"

"No reason. Hey, you introduced Betina to some Warlock?"

"Yeah, he's a good guy, don't worry."

"I worry..." I grumbled and went out the door.

Once back in the car I turned to Annabel who looked very thoughtful. "What do you think we should do?"

"I think we need to keep the stone safe until we have all representatives here," she said simply.

"And the Elves?"

"I guess its time for me to meet my father," she said simply.

Chapter 8

We decided it was best to stash the stone at the Witch's house for now since Annabel had to get some information from her mother anyway. *I* had no interest in going into that house ever again, so I waited outside. The last time I was in there I drank some tea Misty had made and I was falling all over Logan like a horny drunk sorority girl for an hour. It was eye opening and embarrassing at the same time. Who knows what would happen this time? Witches were notorious for nosing their way into other people's business, trying to help where they weren't wanted in pushy ways. They were also absolutely insane.

I could hear the music blasting out of the house from here along with quite a few screeching voices. I leaned against the car, closing my eyes, and soaking up a bit of the rare sunshine.

I heard the growl seconds before I was grabbed and crushed against a large chest. I reached for my pepper spray, but it wasn't there, I must have dropped it on the boat after nearly blinding everyone. "Don't move, don't scream, or I am going to blow a hole in your pretty little side," Kyle growled.

"Why am I not surprised to meet you here, stalking your ex-wife? That's very cliché you know." I couldn't help being sarcastic, I wasn't a fan of being kidnapped and twice by the same dumb Werewolf was incredibly annoying.

He jabbed the barrel of the gun into my side and growled. "Hand over your weapons," he hissed.

"I don't have any today, lucky you," I said between clenched teeth. I couldn't help wondering how long it would take one of the many Witches inside that house to notice I was being harassed in the street.

"Where's your phone?"

"At home," I said with a sigh, I had somehow managed to come out completely helpless and disconnected.

"What the hell is wrong with you?"

I spun around despite his grasp. "Excuse me! *I* am not the one stalking an Ex and trying to kidnap innocent bystanders."

"She is my *wife*! And that is my *child* in there and you are just some bitch I can use for trade. So don't piss me off or I will find someone else."

"Okay, calm down, Kyle."

He growled, showing me his teeth, and they were sharp! "This is about as calm as I'm gonna get, honey."

"So, what's your plan? Drag me in front of the house and expect Tara to run outside, straight into your arms?" I wanted to keep him talking, the last thing I needed was him taking me somewhere alone.

"I'm-I'm going to make Logan give her to me."

"Because Logan is in charge of Tara?" I said with a raised eyebrow and a little shake of the head. "You are clearly not thinking this through, Kyle. Why don't you just walk away, and maybe I can talk to Tara and Logan about the situation. You know I probably make a better ally than hostage." His eyes narrowed, but I could see the wheels turning. "Look, Kyle I don't think there is any reason to make yourself seem more violent at this point. It can only hurt your situation."

"And what do *you* suggest? If I just let you go at this point you'll run and tell Logan that I tried to hurt you, or tell *daddy*, then my life would end I imagine, and my son would grow up fatherless."

"Don't all the Witches grow up fatherless?"

He grabbed my arm and shook me. "That's not the way Werewolves do things!"

"Woah! I get it, Werewolves are traditional. Look, all I'm saying is that I can help you more if you don't shove a gun in my side."

"Fine, you talk to them and set up a meeting. I want to talk to Tara, and I want to see my son."

"Sure, might be good to get some counseling in the meantime because... you're a little angry."

"Counseling," he said suspiciously.

"Yeah, learn to deal with your shit, maybe come to a yoga class too. It will help you align your body and spirit."

"Yoga..."

"Yeah! Trust me, its great for self awareness and control."

"I will be in touch soon," he said and walked away quickly.

Moments later Annabel was by my side. "Did I just see Kyle?"

"Yeah."

"What the hell happened?"

"I convinced him to do yoga."

"Are you okay, Fawn?" Annabel grabbed my arms and looked into my face, concern deep in her eyes. "You aren't making any sense."

I laughed because it was kind of funny really. "I convinced him I will make a better ally than hostage. I told him I would talk to Logan and Tara, but he needs to figure out how to deal with his anger issues, maybe take a yoga class."

Annabel let me go but still looked at me like I was halfway to crazy. "I don't think she wants anything to do with him."

"Yeah well, it kept him from taking me hostage, so I would have said anything. Plus, if he takes my advice and gets some help, it can only be better for everyone."

"Speaking of disastrous Werewolves, yours is at your house and asking where the hell you are. Betina is teaching at the studio, she took Bay and Eldoris with her. I am not sure if he has discovered the Vampire in the basement or not but I imagine Evie spilled that right away."

"Okay," I sighed. "Well let's go put out that fire. How did it go inside?"

"Are you sure you're okay, Kyle's a bit of a creep."

"Yeah, let's go." I jumped into the car.

"I stashed the stone in my room, no one will go in there, I cursed it," she said with a laugh. I looked at her a little worried. "Don't worry, just anyone who enters my room will be immediately slammed with severe bowl discomfort."

"Wow, harsh, remind me never to piss you off."

"Don't go in my room and you'll be fine," she laughed.

"And what did your mother have to say about the Elf clan?"

"My father is Fanlin," she said simply.

"As in the Elf leader that told Eldoris to find me?"

"One and the same. He is apparently aware I exist though he's never tried to contact me."

"You don't have to go there," I said quietly.

"Oh no, I am going. Its long overdue," she said with determination.

"Well, I am with you, as long as that's what you want."

"Definitely, I need the moral support. Might not hurt to take Logan too, Fanlin likes Logan."

"I don't think Logan is about to let me out of his sight so I think he will have to go!" I was a little worried about Logan's tendencies to overprotectiveness, then again, I was attacked twice while he was away for a night so I guess I can't blame him for the worrying. At this point he only knew about the one though.

When we got home Logan barreled out of the front door and nearly knocked Annabel over in his rush to get to me. "What the hell are you thinking leaving the house unprotected and without your goddamn phone!"

"First of all, hi, nice to see you back."

Logan growled, "I don't have the patience for funny, are you alright?"

"Yes, I am fine, and I promised Kyle just now that I would talk to you about how he can deal with his anger and possibly get his wife and child back."

"Just now!" Logan's eyes flashed and I swear I saw his nose start to elongate.

"Calm down, I am fine, obviously. He doesn't want to hurt me, he just wants a hostage, but I convinced him he was better off with me as an ally. So I officially have talked to you about it, you should call him and figure out what should happen from here, but I don't think Tara wants anything to do with him."

"She doesn't," Annabel offered dryly.

"He needs to get out of town, but okay, you survived Kyle. What about everything else?"

I gave him a brief rundown of the events of the last day and a half. He almost lost it a couple more times, especially when I mentioned Dante.

"You're telling me that Dante Vamprose is in your basement right now?" he said with a calm that I knew was worse than his earlier anger. "I knew I smelled Vampire, but I thought perhaps it was just some leftover scent of Drake and Zin."

"What is wrong with Dante?" I asked carefully.

"He's the opposite of Drake, in every way that Drake is kind and fair, Dante is an absolute monster. I wouldn't trust him; I *don't* trust him! Does Drake know he's here?"

"I texted him, but I don't know if he's seen it yet."

"Did he... do anything?" Logan asked carefully.

"No, just asked for a safe place to sleep," I lied. I was sure he had done something, leaking his desire into my mind and body, but I was not going to tell Logan that.

Logan didn't look as relieved as I would have liked, but he didn't press for more. "You should be careful around him."

"Okay, so are you going to go see Fanlin with us? We might need you; he likes you."

Logan looked at the sun, "I suppose we could get there and back before sundown. Tell Betina to keep out of the house until we return."

I retrieved my phone and messaged Betina to stay at the studio all day with Bay and Eldoris, she was dramatic, but agreed.

We piled into Logan's truck and headed out to visit Annabel's father. It was a two-hour drive where Logan grilled me again on everything that had happened, with Kyle at the market, with Dante at the docks, and Jeff at the docks, then Kyle again outside of the Witch's house. He wasn't any more relaxed the second time I told the stories, but he did agree I'd done the right thing, convincing Kyle that I could be an ally. And he couldn't come up with a better option than offering Dante sanctuary in my basement, though he still wasn't happy about it.

"Do you have something personal against him?" Dante had certainly seemed to have something personal against Logan.

"It doesn't matter."

"Excuse me! He is in my basement and you are my-my boyfriend and it certainly does matter!"

Logan's knuckles were white as he gripped the steering wheel. "Fawn, believe me when I say it doesn't matter."

I felt like pouting, and I was definitely *not* going to let it go. But I knew better than to push him too far when he was so irritated.

"What are you going to do about Kyle?" Annabel asked, changing the subject.

"I will set up a meeting with him and my father. It's up to my father from there, I already did what I felt was best. I doubt my father will leave him alive."

I wasn't sure I liked that option, but I didn't know what was best either. He had threatened my life twice, he was obviously unstable. The fact that he had been abusive to Tara was enough to put him on the short list for a death sentence by itself.

Chapter 9

We arrived at a massive silver gate on a backroad, there was a huge blue E on the gate with an intricate emblem behind it. I couldn't see anything beyond the gate, it was so thick with trees. "Subtle," I said. Elves kept so much to themselves I was surprised at such an ostentatious gate guarding their clan.

"Not a lot of people bother down this road," Logan said, and I could imagine that was true, it was well off any main highway to anywhere. He got out of the truck and went to the gate, laying his hand on the emblem, then I heard him say his name in a loud clear voice. He walked back to the truck, and I was ready to call him nuts when the gate separated and opened up.

"Groovy," Annabel said.

We drove through rows and rows of trees for at least ten minutes then it all opened up. A huge meadow and then rows and rows of houses. They all looked like something out of a fairy tale, wood and stone houses with flower gardens and thatched roofs. They were delightful to look at and I couldn't help liking the Elves just a little bit for this delightful neighborhood they'd created. No one was out but I could feel their eyes watching us as we drove, weaving through cobblestone streets and ending at an exceptionally large home in what seemed to be a hill in the center of the community.

Logan parked and we all got out, just standing for a moment, taking it all in. "Do you expect Fanlin will recognize you?" Logan asked.

"I don't know," Annabel said. "Not that it matters, I need his agreement on what to do with the stone, not his recognition."

"Well, let's get to it then," Logan said without an ounce of sympathy.

"Are you ready?" I asked Annabel gently.

"I think I have to be," she said, staring at the house.

I turned to look and saw an Elf standing on the porch. He had white hair that reached his waist and white eyes that looked out of a porcelain face. His lips had a blue tint to them and did not move into any semblance of a smile. He was wearing a white robe over flowing white pants and a white button up shirt. He lifted a hand in greeting but said nothing. His eyes glanced over Logan and I, quickly settling on Annabel. She stepped forward and froze. They stared at each other for what felt like forever.

"Misty's child," he said calmly.

"Yeah, I guess so," Annabel replied with an equal amount of calm.

"You are called?"

"Annabel," she said, taking a small step forward.

"Annabel, I like it. Are you well?" He asked in an awkward way, but it seemed to me that he meant it in a fatherly type of manner.

"Yes, my mother and her coven have taken care of me well."

"And you are here on official business?" he looked back to me and Logan.

"Yes, we have something to discuss. Perhaps inside?" Annabel suggested.

"Of course, come in." Fanlin opened the door.

The house was surprisingly modern considering the outside appearance. Nothing overtly technological, but not a hobbit hole either. Fanlin led us into a living area where we all took uneasy seats. Fanlin watched Annabel carefully.

"Do you have Elf tendencies?" he asked.

"Some, yes," she said, pushing her hair back behind her pointed ears. "I am very good at sniffing out old magic, like Poseidon's stone."

"Poseidon's stone!" Fanlin gasped if you can count the small movement as a gasp. Elves were not overly dramatic.

"Yes, we have located it in the hands of a human. We plan to return it to the sea with the blessing of all the ocean creatures, which includes this colony of Elves I believe."

"We are said to be decedents of a pair of lovers, one Elf and one Siren. It is why we have a connection with the ocean, the tides."

"So can I take the place as Elf representative with your blessing?"

"Of course, daughter. I expect you will keep me updated as to the stone's final resting place."

"I will," she said quietly.

I got the feeling that something more had just passed between the two, as if somehow the promise to keep in touch about the stone was more than politeness. I was happy for my friend, she deserved to know this part of herself. Even if it was weird and basically the exact opposite of how the Witches lived and presented themselves. In every way that the Witches were loud chaos, the Elves were quiet order. Nothing was out of place, no noise was heard other than our own breathing, it was unnerving really. I shifted in my seat anxiously.

"Logan, this mate is well chosen," Fanlin said with absolutely no emotion.

It sent a jolt of emotion through me though. I was filled with anxiety at the word and my face turned beat red. I stared at Logan, imploring him to say something, anything! I tried not to focus on the meaning behind the word *this*. Had there been others to be considered? Did I care? None of these lines of thought were desirable at the moment and I did everything I could to push them down deep.

"She is turning out to be quite the savior of her little slice of the world," Logan said noncommittally.

I was quickly filled with a different kind of anxiety, why wasn't he claiming me as his mate! What the hell Logan! "Logan and I are partners in a sort of way, keeping the peace and solving problems."

"Like the stone?"

"Yes, like the stone."

"So, you are the one who will be in charge of it, until it reaches its final resting place?"

"I-I will be making sure it makes it to its final resting place," I said cautiously. I wasn't planning to keep the thing in my house, and something told me I shouldn't make any false claims to this Elf.

"Very well, I trust you and my daughter as well as Logan. I will put no more thought to the stone. My clan will be happy to know the distress we've all been feeling over the ocean's sickness is about to end. When I sent Eldoris to find you, I wasn't sure you would be successful. We were preparing for an imminent death."

I wasn't sure how to respond to that. The Elves were just going to roll over and die if I hadn't been able to locate the stone! That was a lot of pressure and now the thing was sitting in the middle of the Witch's house mildly protected. "You have nothing to worry about," I said, hoping I sounded more confident than I felt. His white eyes seemed to bear into my soul, and I was sure he was sensing how I really felt. I was thankful he didn't call me out on it.

We left soon after, Annabel and Fanlin shared a brief moment when he reached out and touched her arm lightly, thanking her for coming.

"That was weird," I said when we were driving back through the streets of the quiet community.

"Elves don't show emotions, they feel all of them, from everyone around them, it can be overwhelming I imagine," Logan offered.

"What was he sensing when he called Fawn your mate?" Annabel said with an innocence I didn't buy. I shot her a quick glare.

"I am very protective over Fawn, he must have sensed our connection to each other," Logan said gruffly.

I hoped Annabel would leave it at that. We had a long drive back and a questionable Vampire in the basement to deal with next.

"Has he met other... females you were protective of?" Annabel pressed.

I gritted my teeth. "Annabel, there is no assumption between Logan and I that we are each other's first relationship." I tried very hard to sound like I didn't care how deeply Logan had felt for anyone else. Annabel sat back and left it, damn intrusive Witch, she couldn't help stirring up troublesome thought and feelings.

The whole ride back I worried. I worried about letting down, well everyone. I worried about how committed I was or should be to Logan, how committed he may or may not be to me. I worried about what Dante was in town for, and how would Drake react to my harboring him. I worried about the dark attraction I felt for his damning dimples and salacious remarks. I worried.

We got home a little before dark and luckily Betina had listened and stayed away all day with Bay and Eldoris. "What's the plan?" I asked Logan.

"I am going to talk to Dante. Annabel you should check on the stone."

"Good plan, meet back here at sundown?" I asked.

"Oh yeah, you couldn't pay me to miss whatever this is all going to blow up to," Annabel said with a cheerful laugh. I smiled, this was the girl I knew and loved, she'd been so serious after meeting her father, I'd hate for him to rub off on her too much. She gave me a quick hug and was off on her mission.

I followed Logan into the house. We were met with wagging tails and barks of joy from Pete and Jake. Chester tweeted happily, and Sofia and Jasper meowed demanding *food!* "I missed you too," I said sarcastically as I fed them.

"Oh good, Logan's home!" Evie said, appearing in the kitchen. "Its lonely without you here."

"I missed you too, Evie. Apparently if I leave for a night Fawn brings all kinds of dangerous creatures in to keep her company."

"Oh, the dark handsome stranger in the basement," Evie said fanning herself. "I agree with Fawn, he is yummy!"

"Is that what she said?" Logan said with a growl.

Evie didn't notice Logan's dangerous mood. "Well can you blame her?"

Logan's eyes were on me, and I was trying my best not to react. "Do you want me to go down with you, or..."

101

"I think I will talk to him alone," Logan said gruffly. "I wouldn't want your conflicted feelings getting in the way of a serious discussion," he said through clenched teeth and headed for the stairs.

A few moments later Pumpkin came scrambling up the stairs. I scooped her up and she meowed *dog*. "I know, he's a little irritated." I sat on the couch trying to soothe Pumpkin and waited. When Logan came up, he dropped himself into a chair rather than beside me and I knew something must be really wrong. I sat up and Pumpkin jumped away, rushing off to the basement I assumed. "What is it?"

"Old business."

"But what does—"

"Send another message to Drake. Tell him to be here at sundown."

I scrambled to obey but I still wanted answers. After I sent the message I looked at Logan expectantly. "Don't you think you should clue me in now?"

Logan looked at me and raised one eyebrow, he took a deep breath. "He says he needs help with a problem. He also said that he was attracted to your magic downtown, it took him off his path and brought him to you. There is something he needs from you. Though he wouldn't give me any more details. I have a theory though..."

"From me? What could I possible be helpful with?" I looked toward the basement door and bit my lip. It was nearly impossible for me to resist helping a supernatural, what did Dante need me for?

"I don't know, but I don't like it!"

I looked at Logan and frowned, "You aren't about to forbid me or something like that are you?"

Logan's eyes narrowed, "I might."

"Don't bother, you'll only make yourself look like a fool. I am not interested in a relationship where you make all the rules, Logan. It was never part of the deal."

"And what *is* our deal?" He asked darkly, his eyes revealing nothing but the way his hands were gripping the armrest I knew he was barely holding back.

"What is your old business with Dante?" I countered and we stared at each other, neither one of us wanting to give. I wasn't afraid he would hurt me; I was afraid he was keeping something from me that would hurt us both.

The front door burst open then, stopping all possibility of further conversation. Betina walked in, smiling brightly with Bay and Eldoris following. "Oh Logan! I am so glad you're back!"

"Nice to see you too, Betina," he said quietly.

Introductions were made and the cats came out to sniff and whine about the smell of fish again. "We brought them a treat!" Bay said, holding up a bag. "Some fresh fish from the market."

"You went back to the market!" I said, worried.

"Well we had to, Betina was telling us about the cute boy she met there," Bay confided.

I gave Betina a disapproving look, "I told you to stay at the studio all day."

"As if! That got boring so we went exploring a bit, no big deal. Oh! And Kyle showed up at the studio."

"Kyle!" Logan exploded.

"Yeah, he said Fawn told him to come in for a class. He mostly laid there and stared at the girls, but he tried a little," Betina said brightly. "He did make the girls a little uncomfortable though, he stared and growled a lot, it was a human class."

"Fawn, I don't know what you were thinking," Logan cursed.

"Hey, at least he is trying! I think you should meet up with him, get this figured out. I don't really want him stalking my yoga studio." Now I was mad, I was doing everything I could to keep Kyle from biting my head off, from letting the ocean die, from letting Stephan continue selling magical items to humans, and be hospitable to a very interesting Vampire in my basement. I had about enough of Logan's dirty looks. I glared at him now. "If you had taken care of things the first time, Kyle wouldn't be gallivanting around Seattle trying to kidnap me and hold me for ransom!"

"You want me to take care of Kyle?" Logan yelled. It was so loud the entire house shook, the girls vanished and so did the animals. So much for my protective dogs.

"Yes," I said with a strong calm voice.

"Fine," he said and stormed out.

I didn't start breathing again until I heard his truck peel out and fade down the road. "Whoa, what's he so upset about?" Evie said popping in.

104

"The downfall of male dominance in this household," I said flatly.

"You know dear, a woman's job is to keep her home and man happy. Maybe if you didn't go wandering around the city at night so often like a-a lady of the night, he wouldn't be so angry all the time."

I rolled my eyes at her and tried not to laugh at her insinuation that I was out hooking at night. Though lady of the night was a befitting name for most supernaturals. "Thanks for the advice, Evie."

The girls came back in then. "You really pissed him off," Betina said with wide eyes.

"Don't worry, he'll be back." I was fairly sure. I turned to Bay and Eldoris. "I need you two to go out and bring me a representative from the other ocean clans, can you do that? There needs to be a consensus as to where the stone will be kept safely."

"Of course," they both agreed quickly.

"Betina, drive them down to the empty pier by Lila's bar and wait for them to return." I thought about it for a second. "I don't want you to be alone, maybe you should call Chase."

"Sure!" she said brightly, and they were off quickly to do my bidding.

I fell to the couch and sighed, what was I going to do about Logan? If he acted like an idiot every time my life was in danger, or I was trying to help some male supernatural, we would never survive as partners or anything more.

Chapter 10

It wasn't long before the sun fell far enough for Dante to emerge from the basement. He flashed a dimpled smile my way and his eyes swept the room, then he relaxed a bit. "I thought I heard a fight, did you come to your senses and break things off with that Werewolf? Perhaps you've got your eye on something a little more... sophisticated?"

I ignored his innuendo, "Logan said you need my help."

"True, I wasn't sure when we first met. Something drew me to you at the pier, your magic was calling out to me and I wasn't sure why. I'm still not positive, but I think that you are going to be imperative to my success."

"And Drake?"

"I thought I was coming here for Drake, but maybe I came for you." His blue eyes were intense, hypnotizing almost. He moved closer to me, and I felt my breath catch. "You have strong abilities, don't you sweet Fawn."

"I-I don't think so," I admitted.

"Ah! A lack of confidence, well we shall see if we can do something about that." Dante reached out and stroked a finger down my cheek. "You are a beautiful Magician, and you radiate power, I can sense it. What *are* your known abilities?"

I cleared my throat and blinked my eyes, what was wrong with me? My mind was fuzzy, and my body was hot, being this close to Dante was confusing. "I communicate with animals."

"Yes, I have seen that. Your pets love you."

"I am quite bendy," I said with a giggle. Horrified by the sound, I slapped a hand over my mouth, embarrassed.

Dante only smiled and his eyes intensified. "That could be interesting, what else?"

"I'm an empath, I am drawn to help."

"Yes, I can feel that. There is something more."

"I might have some healing ability." It was something I hadn't explored a lot, but it was probably what had saved Drake's life when he'd been injured and in my basement.

"Yes! Your healing magic is what I must have sensed. I sense it still building within you, Logan does as well. It scares him. He is afraid he will lose you if you don't need him anymore. He is fragile in the way of human men, he feels he must be stronger than his female, needed by her for protection."

My mouth dropped open, could that be true?

A car stopped outside and broke the spell, Dante stepped away and suddenly I felt alone, cold. I looked at him and he just smiled a sexy half smile.

Annabel walked in then, smiling brightly. "Oh good, I didn't miss anything."

"What were you afraid you would miss, my dear?" Dante laughed.

"The brotherly reunion! Where's Logan?"

I frowned. "Off to find Kyle I guess; I don't really know."

"They are having a lovers quarrel," Dante offered.

"Oh, well I am sure it'll be fine, Logan's kind of a hot head."

"Werewolves are unpredictable creatures, only recently housebroke," Dante said with a snicker.

"Is the stone safe?" I asked, hoping to change the subject.

"Oh yes, Catherine tried to go into my room and *borrow* a sweater while I was gone. She became instantly violently ill, so my spell is working and no one else will bother trying now!"

"Great! I sent Bay and Eldoris for the others."

"It seems to me that you are all quite capable, I don't know why Logan doesn't agree," Dante said, slyly bringing the conversation back around.

"How long have you known Logan?" I asked, suddenly remembering their *old* business.

"As long as he has been alive, so not long in comparison to my life, however we've been intricately involved for quite a few years now."

"Involved how?"

"I feel it is Logan's business to tell you, however if I tell it, perhaps I'll have a better chance of winning you over to the pleasure of my company." He had stepped close again and despite the presence of Annabel, the room felt lost, and it was just him and I and I wanted very much to investigate the pleasure of his company.

I was thankful for the sound of another car pulling up to distract from the very wrong turn this conversation had taken. Dante stepped away, Annabel was standing with mouth dropped open and Drake suddenly stood in the doorway, his face set, calm, his eyes piercing into Dante. There was no loving reunion, the air crackled with tension. "Brother," Drake said quietly.

"Father is curious to know why you are still here, I think I understand now." Dante's eyes flicked quickly to the side and there stood Zin.

She was quietly watching the two. "Oh Zin!" I said, trying to break the tension. I rushed forward and pulled her in for a hug. It got the others moving and soon we were sitting uncomfortably in the living room. Pumpkin walked in and hurried to Drake then looked at Dante and walked over to him rubbing against his leg then back to Drake. She was obviously confused as to which was her favorite. Finally, she settled on Drake's lap and he petted her absently. Dante's lip lifted in amusement, seeing his brother with a cat in his lap must have been unusual. It still surprised *me* a bit.

"Why are you here?" Drake asked Dante, his face was still emotionless, careful. "Logan is not—"

"I am looking for Anthea," Dante said, breaking Drake off mid-sentence and I could have screamed, what did this all have to do with Logan? "She is here, and she is hurt."

Drake's eyes widened and he sucked in a breath. Zin held his arm and looked at him anxiously. No one spoke for too long; I couldn't handle it. I was about to say something, anything!

"Who's Anthea?" Evie asked, making me jump. I hadn't even realized she was in the room. Beside me Annabel started too, at least I wasn't the only one put on edge.

"My daughter," Dante said quietly. "She came here to see what was keeping you from returning," he said to Drake, who looked guilty for a brief moment. "She stopped responding to my calls after saying she'd felt the pull of a powerful artifact distracting her from her mission and I can feel her distress. She never even made contact with her fiancé from my understanding."

"Where is Ezra? You two are rarely apart," Drake asked, distracting me from the fiancé question that was swimming around my head.

"He dropped me here and is following a lead farther south."

So that explained why he was on foot when he found me, but who was Ezra?

"Who's Ezra?" Evie asked, not caring at all about being rude with her questions and reading my mind exactly! Sometimes I was really grateful to have her here.

"Our brother," Drake said to no one in particular. "So, what do you need?"

I was surprised by Drake's willingness to help, he had seemed not to like this brother one bit. Of course, he must be worried about his niece. Especially if she were in trouble because she had been looking for him.

"I need Fawn, she is a healer and I need your little love there to get us into some parties I suppose. We need to find out if any locals know anything about Anthea, she was here and responding for a few days, so I know she made some contacts. She was hanging out in the Vampire scene hoping to catch sight of you."

Drake hesitated, I was willing to bet he hated the idea of Zin and me going anywhere with Dante, but I was hooked. I could feel my instincts shouting to help Dante and especially his daughter who was possibly hurt and in my territory too! "What do we do?" I asked.

"Party, ask around and see if anything comes up. So you'll want to put on something sexy," Dante said with a grin and a wink. "That shouldn't be too difficult for you."

"Oh, I am going too!" Annabel said quickly. "I will borrow something sexy."

"Of course! Annabel is great in a crowd; she'll sniff out information." I was glad she wanted to go; it would make it feel a little less like coupling up.

"Where's Logan?" Drake hissed. "Hasn't he returned from Brakemoor?"

"They got in a tiff, and he stormed out," Dante explained. "You know Werewolves are terribly moody and for such a strong-willed female as I can tell Fawn is, they are not very well matched I'd say."

"I suppose you would think that," Drake said quietly.

Zin looked at me, worried. I just shook my head; she relaxed a little. "He's off to find Kyle. Annabel let's go change. Evie, Zin, do you want to help me?" Zin was already dressed for a party in a tight red dress and black heels. Her short hair was sleek tonight, and she had a black choker around her neck. She was carrying a black cape with a red velvet lining, and she looked perfectly the part of Vampire party girl. They followed me up the stairs, giving the brothers a moment alone.

"I don't trust him," Zin said when my bedroom door closed.

"Me neither, but I can feel his distress, its real," I assured them. My instincts were screaming in fact, I had to help Dante. "His daughter is suffering, and we can't ignore that," I added so hopefully they wouldn't think it had anything to do with Dante's sexy smile.

"Do you know anything about him, or Anthea?" I asked Zin.

"No, Drake and I never talk about families."

That didn't surprise me, Zin had been left in the woods, abandoned as an infant and adopted by Werewolves, and Drake had been married before and lost his wife and child to the sun. No doubt they both had family issues that ran deep.

"I think he's cute," Annabel said with a grin.

"What about Logan, what's going on with you two?" Zin demanded.

"Honestly I don't know, he is cranky and controlling."

"Yeah, so what's knew?" Zin said with an eye roll.

"I don't know," I hissed, exasperated. I didn't want to examine it. "Let's just concentrate on finding Anthea."

"Good plan, what are we going to wear?" Annabel said.

I pulled something very vampy out of my closet. Fish net stockings under black leather shorts, chunky boots, and a red velvet corset top. I grabbed a faux fur cape and knew I would fit in at any Vampire club. My hair was loose around my shoulders and I put on some dangly black cross earnings and a choker with a skull on it. "How do I look?"

"You need some of this," Annabel said, handing me a bright red lipstick. She'd chosen a purple leather miniskirt and black corset top. Her own tall black boots, black leather jacket and thick black belt added just the right amount of Witch to the outfit. She'd pulled her hair into a braid down one shoulder. She looked amazing.

"You both look like hookers," Evie said shaking her head.

"Alright, we will fit right in!" I said, smiling at Annabel who was laughing.

"Yes, you both look like real Vampire fan girls. I'm afraid Dante might just eat you up," Zin said with a wink.

I ignored the feelings that were swirling at the thought of what Dante might think of my outfit. I was a Magician, I loved to be flashy, that's all this was about, I tried to tell myself. Besides, I was on a mission, and it required I fit in at the Vampire club. We opened the bedroom door and listened, there was a murmur of voices but couldn't tell what they were talking about. "At least they aren't trying to kill each other," I said.

"Or they are both almost dead and so they can only barely whisper through their ripped bleeding throats," Zin added dryly.

I gave her a patronizing look, "Okay Debbie Downer, I don't smell blood, so let's go." We walked downstairs to find the two men in conversation with bent heads and quiet voices, definitely not trying to kill each other.

They turned our way and Dante rose immediately. "Fawn, you look quite the part. I dare say you'll be drawing a lot of attention wherever we go."

"That's the plan," I said saucily, throwing my cape over one shoulder and striking a pose.

He held out a hand to me as I hit the last step. "May I offer myself as protector of your virtue for the night, in place of Logan?"

"That seems reasonable," I said noncommittally, though the thought had painted a very non virtuous picture in my head.

115

His eyes flashed as if reading my thoughts exactly, then turned to Annabel. "And Annabel! How will I keep you safe too?" Dante smiled at her. I had a moment of jealousy, seeing him throw that dimpled smile in another direction.

"I can take care of myself," she said confidently, and I wished I'd been smart enough to say the same thing.

It seemed best to take two vehicles, since we weren't going to fit comfortably in one. Dante Annabel and I went in my car, Drake and Zin took hers. We were heading downtown, back to the club where I had once been levitated above the crowd. I could be quite sure that wouldn't happen this time, Stefan wasn't dumb enough to still be in Seattle, though if he were it would be mighty convenient.

Chapter 11

We were standing in the cold outside a familiar door, and I could hear the music bumping inside. Dante put an arm around me and one around Annabel and I couldn't help thinking of the last time we'd been in this situation. It had been Logan's unwilling arm around us as we waited to enter the club. When we emerged from the club, he had told me he had feelings for me. In his super cranky way. I probably should have called him before we left the house, but damn if he didn't piss me off with his possessive controlling attitude and secret keeping.

Zin knocked twice, then three more quick raps. It opened and the same tall Vampire I recognized from before, opened the door and let us in. I think he recognized us, but he eyed Dante aggressively as we passed. "Traded up," he said to me as we passed. Well, he didn't exactly say it so much as think it in my direction and I heard it clearly in my head. It was creepy. I eyed him suspiciously, he nodded to Dante. "Not a Werewolf this time."

"Yeah," I thought back, not sure he would hear it. His smile told me he had and I almost giggled. I had just communicated telepathically! That was so cool! It definitely lifted my mood as we walked down the familiar twisting hall, downstairs, and to the club. If that Vampire could push his thoughts into my head in the form of such clear spoken words, could Dante push his feelings and sensual visualizations into mine? I would have to ask Drake about his brother's particular talents. It would be nice to not be responsible for the confusing and scandalous things that have run through my mind since meeting Dante.

The place was packed, same as before, wall to wall bodies moving to the loud music. There was a bar serving mostly blood and an area with couches to rest on. We went to the bar first, three glasses of blood and two glasses of wine.

"I do best alone, so see ya." Annabel walked into the crowd on the dance floor. I wasn't anxious to be alone with Dante, but I didn't want to voice that and seem weak.

"We will circle right, you two circle left," Dante instructed, putting a familiar hand around my waist and guiding me away before anyone could argue. "You're causing quite a stir in here, love. Every male is staring and desiring you as far as I can tell."

I was sure he was exaggerating, but as I looked around, I definitely noticed more than one set of eyes on us. "Maybe they're just wondering what Cassius' sons are doing here."

"Oh, you think our reputation precedes us?" He said thoughtfully.

"Definitely."

"Well, I hope that doesn't inhibit our investigation. I had better do all I can to make them think I am here for pleasure and not business." He moved so fast I had no time to react. He pulled me around and slammed his mouth to mine, his hands moved down to cup my ass and pull our bodies closer. I could feel every inch of him, and my body reacted. His reacted as well, unmistakably pressing against my belly. The heat built first where his mouth moved against mine and then lower, where our bodies melded together in a most delicious way. Then his kiss softened and his hands moved to my hips. I couldn't help parting my lips and allowing the kiss to deepen, he wasn't demanding, he was asking, and I wanted to say yes. When he finally pulled away, I was uneasy on my feet and thankful he didn't let go and let me fall. "I think we fooled them," he whispered, his face still impossibly close to mine.

"Y-yeah," I stammered, trying to remember the point of the kiss. I pushed his hands away and stepped back. "Yeah," I said with a little more force. "So, let's start asking around about Anthea."

We spent three hours in the club making pleasant conversation and casually asking if they'd seen Anthea. We got plenty of confirmation that Anthea had been in town. She had come here a couple times and partied hard, going home with a few different males. Dante didn't seem bothered by the thought, but it made *me* uncomfortable! Wasn't she engaged?

We struck up a conversation with a young Vampire who said he'd hung out with Anthea once or twice while she was in town. He acted like he wasn't going to give any information until Dante revealed who Anthea was. The granddaughter of Cassius Vamprose was certainly someone to keep track of. The boy spilled his guts after that, unfortunately it wasn't very helpful.

"The last night she was here she was talking about some guy she thought might have something. She was really vague about it all but she was definitely worried about whatever it was, said it could be unfortunate for supernaturals. Right before she left, she said something about wanting to check out the Zoo at night. It didn't sound like a good time to me, so I passed, never saw her again."

"You said Anthea was here to find out why Drake hadn't returned, but that wasn't everything, was it?" I asked, pulling Dante to a dark corner. "Time to tell the whole truth." I pressed.

"We got wind of some magical items being sold to humans."

"Like the book on reanimation and Poseidon's stone, yeah I know. Logan and I are investigating, we actually are quite sure we know who it is. We've already set a trap."

Dante looked at me with surprise and respect. "My brother, Ezra, is investigating a report in Portland right now."

"Wait! Is that what you were really doing at the docks, I thought you were drawn to my power." I was offended, and a little hurt, though I really didn't have any reason to be.

"I was there because I sensed the stone and hoped Anthea would be near as well, but when I got close, I sensed you. I knew instantly you would be imperative to my success in finding Anthea."

"And I got the stone," I said with pride.

"You did, you are a very clever girl."

"So, what else do you think was sold?"

"Its impossible to tell. Anyone who had access to the stone would possibly have access to anything. If Anthea thought she had located another object she would have gone after it without thinking and she has no doubt gotten herself into some kind of trouble."

"Where do we start looking?"

"The zoo, Anthea was not an animal lover, there is no reason she'd want to go there unless it was part of the investigation."

"Great...." I hated the zoo, it was depressing. Most of the animals hated it there. When I was in Veterinary school we had to do some classes there and I nearly quit because of it.

Dante looked at me concerned, but I just nodded. I wouldn't let my weakness for animals keep us from helping Anthea.

Deciding to leave was one thing, but actually locating the others was another. I hadn't seen Annabel at all since we'd arrived and the last I saw Drake and Zin, they were cozy on a couch, but as we scanned for them now, I only saw a handful of very amorous young Vampires on the couches who should probably think of leaving and getting a room before things went any farther.

"We only have a couple hours until sunrise, let's hit the zoo, they have another car to get home with," Dante suggested.

I didn't love the idea of being completely alone with him, but I didn't want to admit it to him of all people, so what choice did I have? "Sure," I gritted out and we headed through the crowd for the door. Once in the car I saw I had a message from Logan, but I wasn't ready to talk to him, so I ignored it. Nothing from Betina yet, so she must still be waiting for the girls to return. I gave Dante a quick peripheral glance as I drove us through the dark streets. He didn't look as worried as I could feel rolling off of him, but there was a slightly strained look to his face. He loved his daughter, and he definitely didn't want to find her hurt, or worse. Whatever was between Dante and Drake, or Dante and Logan... I knew Dante wasn't all bad.

"There will be security to deal with," I said as we parked a block away from the zoo and started walking.

"Cameras and sensors?"

"Yeah, any ideas?"

"Guards?"

"I think so, night guard probably sitting in the office watching cameras."

"Wait here, I will be right back." Dante walked off into the shadow and disappeared, leaving me to wait in the shadows of the parking lot.

I watched and waited with no idea what he could possibly be doing, and seriously hoping it wasn't going to involve killing the guard. I shivered and looked at my phone. Should I see what Logan wanted? Should I tell someone I am here with Dante, just in case?

"We are good to go."

Dante's voice made me jump and scream and reach for my nonexistent stun gun or pepper spray. He held up his hands and laughed.

"Woah, jumpy for a supernatural."

"Yeah well, my teeth aren't as sharp as others'" I said quietly.

"Luckily your instincts are to attack first and ask questions later," he joked and I had to smile because he knew exactly what I was capable of, if I had a stun gun.

"So, what did you do?" I asked carefully.

"I convinced the guard to take a nap and turn off the security system. We can walk in and around unnoticed." He looked at me and gave a half smile before adding, "I didn't hurt him."

I braced myself before we went in, the distress of the animals hit me hard. It was like a wave of despair and need crashing over me, I nearly collapsed. I fell against the gate gasping and clutching my chest.

"Fawn, what's wrong?" Dante came close, his voice full of concern.

"I just need a minute, the animals."

Dante looked around, confused. "What animals?"

"Just give me a second, I'll be okay." I closed my eyes and pulled myself together. "Okay, I'm okay."

"Are you sure, I can go on alone."

"No, I've got this." I wasn't completely sure that was true, but I wasn't going to tell him that.

"Let me help you," he said quietly and touched my chin, forcing my eyes to meet his. They swirled and I was lost, falling into them. "Let it go," he whispered. "Let their suffering go, you are not meant to help them today."

His words were like a shot of pain killer, I was suddenly fine, all those feelings of hurt, torment and longing for release from cages and chains was gone. "That was amazing," I drawled, feeling a little drunk.

"It won't last forever, but you should be okay while we need to be here."

I met his gaze again and this time only saw kindness, he was definitely not all bad. "Any idea what Anthea might have been here to look at?"

"Unfortunately no."

We walked by cage after cage of sleeping or pacing animals, but I didn't sense anything off and neither did Dante. It seemed like maybe we'd wasted our time, maybe she'd just come here to see the animals, as unlikely as Dante thought that was. We stopped outside of the bat exhibit.

"This is the last one," Dante said, with little hope in his voice.

124

"Look!" I pointed to the lock; it was broken. We'd had to pick locks everywhere else in here. Luckily, Dante was talented at just such a thing, but this one had been destroyed it looked like, ripped open by someone not caring at all about leaving a trail. We exchanged a surprised look and snuck in. There was nothing immediately amiss, no sense of a human near, or Vampire other than Dante. There was plenty of activity though, the bats hunted and played in their dark enclosure.

We walked further in and Dante froze in front of an office door. "Do you smell that?"

All I could smell was guano, and it wasn't pleasant. I shook my head but leaned closer to the door and sniffed. "Nothing," I admitted unhappily.

Dante picked the lock and we entered a messy office and medical space for the bat keepers. Once inside I was pretty sure I smelled what Dante had. It was faint, like it had been gone for a while now, but when it had been here it'd been so strong that its residue lasted. "What is that?"

"Very old magic." Dante frowned and searched around but came up empty handed.

"I'll see if the bats know anything." I went back out and looked into the enclosure, waiting for a curious bat to come my way. A huge fruit bat swooped down and sat on a nearby branch. "Hello," I said quietly. The bat just looked at me and flew away. "Thanks for the help," I grumbled.

"You were expecting conversation?" Dante asked, coming up behind me.

"I was hoping for something." Another bat, a small one this time, swooped down and landed on the branch looking at Dante.

Her! It screeched. *Love!*

"What about her?" I asked.

It screeched, *cage!* Sadly, and flew away.

"Cage?" I wondered aloud.

"Must be sad to be here, like everything else."

"Yeah, I will come back in the day. Maybe I can get a feeling off the workers. Someone here is doing something they shouldn't, I am sure."

"I'm sorry I can't help with that, but I can follow any lead once the sun goes down. Don't go after the human yourself, or the artifact, it would be too dangerous."

"We'll find her," I reassured, more confident than ever now. If she'd been here and after whatever was in that office, I'd know it as soon as I got close to the human who had it. The only problem was, would they recognize the magic in me too? How much a human knew made them extremely dangerous.

We drove home and found Drake, Zin, and Annabel waiting anxiously outside. Annabel and Zin looked at me curiously, Drake glared at his brother. "What the hell, why did you two take off without us?"

"We couldn't find you and we didn't want to waste time, we had a lead to follow," Dante explained harshly.

"A lead!" Zin said happily. "We had no luck at all."

"Yeah, she had told someone she was going to the zoo. We went and looked, there was definitely something old and magical in the offices of the bat exhibit. I will go back when it's open and see what I can figure out from the humans."

"I'll tag along," Annabel offered.

"The bat exhibit," Drake said, very worried.

"What is it?" I asked when he didn't elaborate.

"Anthea has morphing powers like my mother. She can turn herself into a bat. You're certain she wasn't trapped in there? As unlikely as that seems," Drake said.

"I would have known right away if she were there," Dante scoffed.

I glared at him, that was a bit of information I could use! Why was he acting like I wasn't an important part of this investigation? As if he didn't really want me to be able to find her, at least not without him.

"We will be back tonight to help," Zin said and gave me a tight hug. "Call Logan," she whispered in my ear, and I nodded. I wasn't going to stay mad at him forever, as long as he didn't stay cranky forever.

Zin and Drake left then, and Annabel promised to be back in a few hours so we could get to the zoo early. I looked at Dante and frowned. "You should have told me that Anthea could be a bat."

"It didn't seem important for you to know," he said casually and walked into the house.

I followed quickly, angry now. Evie met us and so did the animals. I was eased from my anger by the onslaught of love and happiness I felt from these animals, so much different from the stress at the zoo.

"You came back!" Evie said happily to Dante.

"Of course, love. I enjoy sleeping the day away in your basement."

Evie giggled.

"Can I get tucked in?" he asked, looking at me meaningfully.

I narrowed my eyes, he wasn't all bad, but he was definitely bad for me. "I think you're a capable man."

Dante laughed, "I suppose I can take care of myself." The way he said it made me think he might be taking care of himself in a very hands-on way. His eyes swept down my now hot body and I knew exactly what he would be thinking about too. "You know where I will be if you want me," he said meaningfully and disappeared into the basement.

"Such a nice man," Evie commented, having completely misread the exchange as usual.

I could barely tear myself away from the spot I was rooted, my eyes glued to the now closed basement door. What did he think, that I would run down after him and happily jump him despite my involvement with Logan? I shook myself out of the thought that was quickly becoming a desire.

"Yeah... has Betina returned?"

"No, that girl is out running wild, I think you're a bad influence on her."

"Maybe," I agreed and took myself off to bed before I made any bad decisions. I looked at my phone and finally checked the message from Logan, feeling guilty.

Found Kyle outside the Witch's house. Taking him to Brakemoor, might be gone for a couple days... be careful! I care deeply for you...

I wasn't sure what to think of *that!* Or how to respond without yelling, so I didn't. I fell asleep annoyed with all the men in my life. My dreams were disturbingly sensual and starred Dante. I dreamed I was walking downstairs in a red lace nightie and finding him naked, lounging in the chair. He motioned for me to join him, and I hurried over, placing myself onto his lap, feeling his obvious desire pressed against me. I moaned as I offered him my neck. He groaned, showing his fangs and dropped his head to pierce the soft skin of my breast.

I woke up panting, sweating and desperately feeling around for bite marks and drips of blood on my chest. I was afraid to sleep after that, I was certain Dante was sending his fantasies into my mind. I managed to slip back into dreamless sleep not long before my alarm was going off.

Chapter 12

The next morning, I snuck out of the house early. Betina was home, and asleep, Chase was crashed on the couch, but there was no sign of Bay, Eldoris, or any other ocean supernaturals. Even Evie was out of sight, so I was able to feed the animals quickly and get out without conversation. I pulled into the yoga studio happy to forget myself for a few hours in a hot room with quiet music.

"Good morning, Sara," I said to the human girl who was running the front desk today.

"Fawn! I am so glad you're here, did Betina tell you about the creep we had in here yesterday?" She shivered a little

"Yeah, she told me. Don't worry, he won't be in again." Sara looked like she wanted to ask why I knew that, but she didn't. She was smart for a human, she sensed something was off about me and

Betina and some others, but she had enough self preservation instincts to not ask.

Annabel was waiting outside the studio when I was done a couple hours later, and we headed to the zoo. I'd showered and dressed after my classes and felt fresh and ready to take on this mystery.

"How was your short night?" Annabel asked, and I know she meant what had happened with Dante.

"Fine."

"And did you talk to Logan?"

"He messaged, he has taken Kyle to Brakemoor, you can tell Tara that he will likely not be seen again, ever."

Annabel nodded, a little sullen. Death was not to be disrespected, but sometimes it was necessary to the good of the many. "Do we have a plan?" Annabel asked, changing the subject.

"Just to hang around the bats, act interested, and hope to find someone who has the smell of old magic clinging to them."

"Easy plan."

"Have you ever heard of a Vampire able to invade your mind?"

"Well they glamour humans, so they can feed forgetably."

"I know that, but I am talking about thoughts, feelings... dreams projected into the mind even."

"That would be a very powerful gift."

"Dangerous."

"Very," Annabel said thoughtfully and gave me a worried look.

I smiled as I drove, "Don't worry Annabel, I am in control of myself, I just wondered." She didn't press, but I knew she could feel my deep concern.

Today we had to pay to get into the zoo and I was thankful there wasn't a police force milling around and investigating a murdered night guard. I never did check on the human to make sure Dante hadn't killed him, I was afraid of what I would find. I was struck again by the animals' despair as we made our way through the zoo. It was overwhelming, Annabel touched my shoulder and the crushing weight of it eased a bit. It wasn't as complete as Dante's magic had been, but it helped.

"Thanks," I sighed.

"Of course," she said simply, as if it were no big deal.

She gave me a wink, her Elf side made her sensitive to other's emotions, I wondered how much she felt when I was so overwhelmed.

We went straight to the bat exhibit and waited, watching, and listening as we pretended to be interested in the bats. A young blonde man dressed like an employee rushed through and yanked open the door to the office we'd been in last night.

"I'm here Shane! I was asleep when Gina called me in," the young man yelled. Annabel flicked a finger and the door jammed open just enough to make their conversation heard without being obvious.

"God damn Travis, how the hell is he still sick!" another man yelled.

133

"Because he's an idiot, says he got bit by that big bat that flew through here."

"Rabies test came back negative."

"She should fire him at this point, he's probably sitting on his couch whacking off to the discovery channel."

"He kept it you know."

"The bat?"

"Yeah, you know that old cage he had hanging over his desk? He caught it in there and took the damn thing home."

"Fucking weirdo."

The young blonde came back out and started sweeping. Annabel and I descended on him immediately. "What can you tell us about these cool bats?" I asked.

"Not much, I am only filling in. I usually work with the cats," he said without looking up.

"Cats are great," Annabel said, drawing his attention. He froze, locked into her mesmerizing gaze.

"Great..." he said groggily.

"Where does your coworker, Travis live?"

It was so easy it was almost ridiculous. Human minds were so easily manipulated, that was probably why they were so susceptible to making poor decisions based on fear. He spilled his guts, not only did we learn where Travis lived but also that this boy held a secret crush on him. He often watched him from afar wishing Travis would look at him the way he looked at the bats. We hurried back to the car, neither of us speaking until we were inside.

"So, what now?" Annabel asked.

"I don't see any reason to wait, if Anthea is in danger waiting until dark is just stupid. We know we can handle a simple human." I pulled out my stun gun and pepper spray.

Annabel smiled. "Yes, we can!"

We pulled up to an apartment building that looked like it had been built in the sixties and never updated. There were outside stairs going up four flights and according to the boy at the zoo, Travis' apartment was on the fourth floor.

"Good thing I wore my All Stars," I said with a sigh, strapping my stun gun and pepper spray onto my belt. I was wishing I could have asked Lila to meet us, she's great for added muscle, but I didn't want to answer questions about why Logan wasn't here. Besides, if Travis was alone, we shouldn't have any problem.

"Just try not to blind all of us this time," Annabel said with a laugh.

"No promises."

We got out and started making our way to the top floor, number 407. I knocked; we were going to just invite ourselves in quickly if he answered. We waited, nothing. I knocked again.

"Maybe he isn't home," Annabel said hopefully.

Annabel picked the lock and went inside. I was going to have to have someone teach me how to do that. Inside it was what I would expect from a human bachelor living in this kind of building. Sparse furniture that looked like it belonged on a street corner, dishes and take out containers everywhere. Laundry in piles and the smell of desperation.

"Boys are gross," Annabel grunted as she kicked a pair of dirty underwear out of the way.

"Yes, yes they are. But can you smell that?"

"Smells like ass and sweat."

"Beyond that, its old magic!" We made our way through the tiny living room and opened a door into the bedroom. It was dark in there, blackout curtains on the small window but my eyes adjusted quickly, there in the corner was a large lump under a blanket, I was drawn to it. I rushed over and ripped the blanket away. A hiss came from inside a large old brass birdcage. *Light!* The hiss said and I covered it back up. "I think its her!" I said excitedly. A Vampire in bat form was still sensitive to the light of the sun apparently. "We need to get her out very carefully." The last thing we needed was to arrive home with a birdcage full of dead Vampire ash.

The bedroom door slammed behind us, and we were plunged into darkness. "That belongs to me."

Annabel clapped and a light burst from her hands, for just a moment I could see him, Travis was standing blocking our exit. He looked surprised by the sudden burst of light but not scared and I was filled with fear. What if he wasn't a simple human after all. He held up something and then the world went black again, only this time it wasn't just my eyes, my mind darkened and I was falling.

Consciousness came back slowly; it was dark and it smelled bad. I was still in Travis' apartment. "Annabel?" I whispered. She groaned beside me. I

136

reached out and touched her, gently shaking her. "Annabel."

"Fawn?"

"Yeah, are you hurt?"

"Only my pride, that fucker had some serious power," Annabel hissed.

"Yeah, do you think he's supernatural?"

"No, I think he bought more than a cage from Stefan." Annabel snapped her fingers, and a small light filled the room. Brief, but long enough for us to see we were on the bedroom floor. I scrambled to the door and listened. "Nothing."

Annabel switched on the overhead light. The cage was gone, and I was betting so was Travis. "Damn!" We had really messed up. "Maybe we should have waited for sundown, no way he would have been able to take us and three Vampires.

A thirty second search of the apartment confirmed it. "I think its time to call in a tracker, Lila's the best I know." I pulled out my phone and called her. She was on her way immediately, so we waited and searched for anything else that might link to supernaturals or a clue to where he might have gone.

"He's got quite the collection of literature on Vampire Bats by his bed, and a stack of very old porn magazines." Annabel came out of the bedroom looking horrified. "I feel like I need a shower in Lysol," she shivered.

"How does a human go from Vampire Bats to a magic cage that traps an actual Vampire in bat form?"

"Good luck?"

"Maybe...." We kept searching but came up empty handed aside from a little white business card with an S on it, Stefan. "I'm really starting to get annoyed by that idiot."

Chapter 13

Lila arrived and we explained everything as quick as we could. "Why isn't Logan here helping?"

I frowned. "He's at Brakemoor taking care of Kyle."

"They had a fight," Annabel offered as further explanation.

"My brother can be an ass, but I know he cares for you, Fawn. More than I've ever seen him care for a girlfriend before."

"Yes, well, one problem at a time. Can you track this asshole before he gets too far?"

"Of course! Try to keep up," Lila said with a wink. She undressed and shifted quickly, then took off out of the apartment, down the stairs and across the street.

Annabel and I grabbed her clothes then hopped into my car and followed as best we could. Lila was sticking to shadows for the most part and we lost her twice, but she circled back and found us again. She led us into a really nice neighborhood with large family homes and manicured lawns. I was sure she'd gotten it wrong when she stopped in front of a cute little house with a picket fence and a flower garden. There was a beat-up truck in the driveway that looked out of place enough to give me pause.

"Do you think it's his girlfriend's place?" Annabel asked.

"I think its his grandmother's place," I said dryly, having flashbacks to entering Ben's mother's house. We drove past and parked in a lot near a neighborhood park. Lilia yelped from the bushes. "I suppose she wants her clothes," I laughed and rushed over to hand them to her. She shifted and dressed quickly. She was good, must have done it a hundred times, it was so fast I don't think anyone would have a chance to notice the naked woman in the bushes.

"How sure are you?" I asked once she emerged.

"The scent was strong, I'm sure. What's the plan?"

"Well, he's seen *us,* so you'll have to be the one to knock on the door. Maybe your car broke down and you need to use the phone?"

Lila laughed, "Isn't that what I told Ben? Do you think it'll be that easy without Logan this time to burst through a wall and knock the boy down?"

"Let's just hope there isn't a dead woman watching tv this time! Annabel and I will wait nearby, if you can get in and confirm that the cage is

140

in there, then we'll figure out how best to get it out. We just *have* to be sure. We can't afford to make any mistakes."

"Sounds good, I will charm my way in." She pushed up her breasts and I knew her *charms* would be very helpful with Travis.

I handed her my stun gun. "Just in case."

Lila rolled her eyes. "I would rather shift and rip his throat out if he tries to harm me."

"He might be expecting that, he knocked us out so fast we couldn't even react. But something as human as a stun gun might surprise him," I reasoned.

She took it and shoved it into her coat pocket, but she didn't look convinced that she'd need it. Annabel and I moved into position near enough to see the front door clearly and hear a shout. If necessary, we would rush in, no way was Lila going to get hurt over this.

"Something smells fishy," Annabel said as we watched Lila knock on the door.

"I agree, something's off."

"No, literally, I smell fish!"

The door opened and there stood Jeff! "Oh my god! The fisherman!"

"This is too weird."

But in a way it made perfect sense. If Jeff and Travis knew each other why wouldn't one tell the other about this great way to get real magical items. One with a penchant for fish, another obsessed with bats, or Vampires... or just Vampire Bats, I wasn't really sure.

My phone rang but I didn't recognize the number. I almost didn't answer it but then realized Lila might be calling from inside! "Hello."

"Hey, it's Lila. My car broke down by the park, can you come pick me up and bring a new battery?"

"Sure thing," I said as calmly as possible. "I will be right there."

"Thanks babe." She hung up and moments later she was walking back out, this time I could see both men and I definitely saw a resemblance.

"Brothers no doubt," Annabel said, seeing the same thing. We hurried back to the park and waited for Lila to catch up.

"It's definitely in there," she said when we were all settled in my car.

"Yeah, we know the guy who answered the door. We stole Poseidon's stone from him the other day."

"Woah! Seriously! That's awesome. Is that what the naked wet woman was after when she walked into my bar looking for you?"

I smiled; it was pretty awesome. I had to admit I was feeling pretty darn good about my P.I. abilities lately. "Yep, octopus shifter. Did you see anything in there or just sense it?" I asked.

"I just sensed it, I didn't go farther than the entryway and they weren't inviting. They were very cautious, but I don't think they suspected anything by the time I was leaving."

"Good, we will go back tonight. Drake and Dante should have no trouble getting in and out with the cage."

"Especially if we set up a convenient distraction," Annabel suggested with a grin.

"Oh, that sounds fun!" Lila clapped.

I wasn't so sure.

We delivered Lila back to her car and went to my house hoping to get some news from Betina. I checked my phone nervously when we pulled into the driveway. I was a little hurt that Logan hadn't said anything today, how long was he planning to stay gone and what were they doing with Kyle?

Betina was eating cereal on the couch when we got in, Chase was gone, and the animals were all asleep. Evie popped in right away then looked disappointed. "When is Logan coming back, I miss him."

"Nice to see you too, Evie," I said sarcastically. She just huffed and disappeared again. "What's the news Betina?"

"Chase and I waited at the bar all night, but they never came back."

It worried me but there wasn't anything I could do about it now. "If they don't show up by morning, we'll... do something."

"Great plan," Betina said sarcastically.

Annabel left with the promise of returning at sunset.

"I suppose I should go to let Dante know what we found."

"I'm going to the studio to teach this afternoon."

"Betina you're amazing. What would I do without you?"

"I don't know," she said with a wink.

I descended the stairs and found Dante lounging with a book. "Fawn! So nice to see you in the day. I must say it's quite difficult to remain alone all day. I don't sleep much." His eyes swept me from head to toe and I had a very clear idea of what he would like to do all day.

I shook off the heat he ignited in me and kept my distance. His eyes lit up and I knew he was enjoying my discomfort. "I found Anthea."

"My daughter! Where is she? Did you bring her here? Is she okay?"

"She is alive, I don't know if she's hurt. We were knocked out by something magical and lost her, then tracked her again. She's being held in bat form in a cage that is no doubt enchanted to keep her from shifting or escaping. We tracked him when we woke up and we confirmed the presence of the cage in a house. We can go tonight and fetch her without problem, I'm certain."

Dante smiled and relaxed slightly. "Very good, you have certainly proven yourself a worthy investigator. Perhaps my father will rely on your services in the future, for problems in the area. Rather than sending Anthea or I again. Of course that would render Drake's position here completely useless."

The thought of dealing with Cassius scared the shit out of me. "Th-thanks," I stammered, knowing better than to turn down an offer from a Vamprose. "Will Drake be forced to leave Seattle?" I was now very concerned for my friends and their future together.

Dante raised an eyebrow. "Drake was never meant to have a permanent place here."

"Why?"

"He is useful to our father, keeping order throughout the large territory he holds. We all work for him."

"But what if he wanted to stay here?"

"That's not his choice to make."

I frowned, I didn't understand, and I was afraid my friend was going to be taken from me, and Zin! Poor Zin would lose her love. "It doesn't seem fair."

"Why do you reside here, Fawn? Why Seattle? Why this territory?"

"Because—" I stopped, knowing exactly what he was getting at. "Because it is my father's territory and I am in charge of this parcel, keeping order here. It is what I was born to do," I admitted grudgingly.

Dante smiled. "My father trusts my judgment; I am his eldest son. If I were to say that Seattle is in need of a permanent representative of the family, he would agree, and Drake could stay."

My face brightened, there was hope. "And will you?"

"Its still a bit before I dare come upstairs, would you like to be a good hostess and entertain me?" His words were thick, and my body heated.

I could imagine just what he might do with those sharp teeth of his and it was dangerously intriguing. Remembering my dream from this morning I shivered with desire. Was he trying to make me exchange myself for Drake's freedom? I loved Drake like a dear friend, but that was too much to ask. I backed away until my feet hit the bottom stair. "I don't mean to be a bad hostess, but I don't think I should."

"Do you always do what you *should*, Fawn?"

"Y-yes," I stammered.

"That's not true, if that were true you would be an extremely poor P.I. because being a real investigator takes the guts to do things you know are wrong. Things that might get you or other people hurt while trying to solve your mystery. So, I ask you again Fawn, do you *always* do what you should?"

While he spoke he'd crossed the room and was now standing directly in front of me, his last words were a whisper that sent a chill down my spine while his sweet hot breath fanned my face. I remembered how that mouth felt on mine, how it tasted, how it made my knees weak and my head spin. I leaned forward; I couldn't stop myself. His hands went to my waist and pulled my body against his and our mouths met in a frantic and hot kiss.

Somewhere in the back of my mind I knew this was wrong, but I couldn't stop myself. There was nothing I wanted more than Dante in this moment, nothing. I hopped and he caught me as I wrapped my legs around his waist, he easily held me there. I held his head as our mouths mated. My tongue slid over his perfect white teeth and hit his incisor, extended and razor sharp. It sliced my tongue, and I was slammed back to reality as my blood dripped into his mouth.

I pulled back and stared into his eyes. They were swarming with something beyond desire, and I could only imagine it had to do with my blood that had dripped onto his tongue. "I think I better go upstairs," I said, breathless.

He hesitated only a second before setting me gently to my feet. "I have no desire to cause you trouble, Fawn. I have lived a long time and I know what I want, and I take it, I want you." His mouth twisted up into a sexy half smile. "I am also very patient, I'll wait."

I didn't know how to respond to that, and I didn't trust myself to say anything in that moment. I turned and hurried upstairs. Then all the way up the stairs to my room and threw myself on the bed. "What the hell is wrong with me?"

"Where should I start?" Evie said popping in. I threw a pillow at her, and she disappeared.

Chapter 14

I woke at sunset to a text message from Logan. *Kyle ran north, don't expect to see him in Seattle again, if he does, he knows he's dead. Be back by morning.*

I responded *K see you soon.*

I showered and dressed in all black. My hair was pulled back in a ponytail, and I made sure I had my stun gun and pepper spray in my pocket. I was ready to take on Jeff and Travis, what I wasn't ready for, was facing Dante. The way I had acted was humiliating and as much as I wanted to blame it on some kind of Vampire mesmerization, I knew it was all me. I was attracted to him, and I didn't want to be but there it was. Undeniable. I still had all the feelings for Logan, I knew I was well on my way to falling in love with him. The last thing I wanted to do was throw it away on a fling with a Vampire who couldn't care less for me. I held no illusions that

Dante cared for me, he wanted me, he'd said as much. But that was lust, which had its place, sure. It just wasn't something to give up love for.

"Can I come in?" Zin asked, knocking on my bedroom door, and breaking me out of my self loathing thoughts.

"Of course," I answered, not that it mattered, she had already opened the door and walked in. "I was just getting psyched up for tonight."

"I thought maybe you were avoiding your houseguest."

"That too, he's... intense."

"Yeah, Drake said he's always been a bit of a dark spirit, very self gratifying and wanton. I think if I'd met him first, he would have been more my type," she giggled. "But of course, I am all sorts of in love with Drakie."

I laughed, thinking of anyone calling a Vampire anything that ended with 'ie. "Is Annabel here too?"

"She was just pulling up when I came up the stairs, so yep, lets go do this!"

I wanted to tell Zin to wait, to tell her that Dante was here to collect Drake and bring him home to their father, but it wasn't my place. I had no doubt that Drake knew, it was his place to talk to Zin about it and if he hadn't, then he must have his reasons. I would just keep out of it, especially since I wasn't offering my services in exchange for him staying.

I followed Zin downstairs and refused to look at Dante as we made our plan. Annabel was there with two of her coven sisters, Jackie and Meriana. They were all dressed in mini skirts and cropped sweaters.

They would be an important part of our plan of distraction. Lila was waiting in the living room as well; she'd picked up some cookies to deliver as a thank you for letting her use their phone. This would have to work!

We all parked at the park and separated to carry out our duties. Drake and Dante went around the back of the house. Lila, Jackie and Meriana headed to the front with their tray of cookies. Annabel, Zin, and I were stationed around the sides of the house watching for any need that may arise.

The plan was, Lila would ring the bell and offer the cookies as a thank you for letting her use the phone. Jackie and Meriana would start making out behind her, drawing the attention of whoever answered, and hopefully he would call the other to the door to watch as well. This would leave the house essentially empty so Drake and Dante could sneak in the back, find the cage, and exit quickly. When they were free, we would whistle and alert the girls who would make a quick exit and we would meet up again at the park. It was a good plan!

From where I was watching behind a neighbor's tree, I could see the front door and the side window. Lila knocked loudly, holding the tray of cookies at breast level. She'd worn jeans and a t-shirt that was low cut and revealed her ample cleavage very nicely.

A young woman answered the door, and we all froze, this was entirely unexpected. If anything, we thought maybe an older woman, their mother or grandmother. We'd planned for that, thinking Lila could ask to talk to her son, to thank him. It could have still worked.

"May I help you?" the woman asked in a weird, monotone sort of voice that sent a panic up my spine.

"I made some thank you cookies for the men here, are they home?" Lila asked.

The woman turned slowly, too slowly; something was definitely wrong with her. "Jeff, someone is here to see you," she slurred.

Jeff came forward and pushed her behind him, eyeing the area behind Lila and the girls cautiously. "Can I help you?"

"I brought you cookies!" Lila said, shoving the plate at Jeff so hard he stumbled back just a bit. "To say thank you for letting me use your phone."

This wasn't the plan; she was being too aggressive. I moved closer. Jackie and Mariana held hands and flanked Lila, but they didn't enact their part either.

"Thanks," Jeff said and tried to shut the door.

Lila was strong though and she put out a hand easily stopping the door from shutting. "Sounds like a party, why don't you invite us in."

"No thanks, we have enough company." Jeff tried again to shut the door, but Lila forced her way inside and that was my cue, I ran for the door as well and caught it just as it was about to close behind Jackie.

"What the hell is going on?" I yelled.

"This asshole has a human girl mesmerized, I can smell the goddamn magic," Lila said, and she had her hand on Jeff's throat. Jeff was coughing and

152

sputtering as he ripped at her hand futilely. Jackie and Mariana went to the girl who'd opened the door and rushed her outside.

"You bitch!" Jeff gasped, recognizing me right as Travis rounded the corner.

"What the—" Travis said, then turned as if he were going to run the other way. I grabbed my stun gun fast and jumped at him, I would have missed by a mile, but Zin came flying in from the other way and knocked him onto me. I made contact and he was down and out and pissing himself. Unfortunately, he was on top of me and I could feel the warm wetness passing onto my own pant leg.

"Oh god get him off me!" I screamed. Drake was there a second later throwing Travis off me.

"What about him?" Lila asked, still holding onto Jeff's throat.

I was mad now, I stunned him until his eyes rolled into the back of his head and he slumped to the ground. "Asshole," I spat. I looked at Drake and Zin, concerned. "We are looking for more than the cage. That human was out of her mind, and it has to be some kind of magic, probably whatever Travis used in the apartment to knock me and Annabel out earlier."

"On it!" Zin rushed off, Drake right behind. Lila and I tied up the two perverts.

"We got the girl fixed up, she'll have an awful hangover, but I think she's fine," Annabel said, coming inside.

"Any idea what they were using on her?" I asked.

"This," Drake said, coming into the room with a bright red stone set in silver. It was about the size of my palm and swung from a thick silver chain.

"What is that?" I whispered, a little in awe of the beautiful thing.

"Its an amulet that lets one control the minds of others, a pretty simple thing really, charmed by Witches and just as easily undone." Drake handed it to Annabel. "I assume your coven can take care of deactivating that."

"Definitely."

"Where's Dante? Did he find the cage? Anthea?" I asked with concern, it shouldn't be that hard, the house was small.

"He already took her out the back, he's meeting us at your place. Fawn, she needs medical attention."

I nodded, ready to do anything I could to save her. I called my father as we drove back to my place. I wanted him to get a more thorough sweep of the house and Travis' apartment. I didn't want to be overly confident this time. I'd left things half done at Ben's house and it could have been disastrous. Luckily, we had a few of our own on the police force for just such an occasion as that was.

"What about the humans?" I asked after relaying all the information. "They haven't broken human laws, the police won't take care of them, but we can't just let them walk around knowing about us!"

"I will send Misty, she can spell them to forget everything, no worries of it *ever* returning," he said confidently.

"Thank you!" I hung up, confident that my father would take care of the loose ends.

When we stopped in front of my house I ran inside and rushed down the stairs when I didn't see Dante in the living room. Jake and Pete looked at me curiously as I hurried through the house. Chester was on Pete's back and tweeted a greeting I ignored.

I found Dante leaned over the cot not moving. "I'm here," I whispered, touching his shoulder gently. He didn't turn but moved aside slightly so I could see. He had laid her out on the bed. Still in bat form, she had her eyes closed and she was breathing rapidly. "I don't know much about bats, and even less about Vampires turned into bats." I didn't want him to be overly confident in my abilities here.

"You have a natural healing power, Fawn. I know you can help her." Dante spoke with such conviction I felt a bit of his confidence leak into me. I *would* do everything I could.

"Get some blood," I ordered. He hurried off and I didn't care too much where he found it, this girl needed it, badly. Then I turned to the bat. I poked gently and turned the small thing in my hand but couldn't see anything outright wrong with her. It was likely only due to lack of blood and the magic of the cage and amulet he'd had. I looked around; the cage was in a corner. I went over to investigate closer. It looked so unassuming. It could have sat in an antique store for years collecting dust, nothing about it indicated it was useful for anything magical. Of course, my own father forged similar items; cages and shackles that no supernatural could get out of.

He always left his mark though, so I was sure there would be something similar on this one. It took me a minute, but I found it, a tiny maker's mark on the inside of the lock, MM.

I sat back, a little stunned, Markus Malero? Had my father built this cage? I pulled out my phone and called my father again. A quick conversation confirmed he'd built the cage and it would definitely keep a supernatural inside but would in no way cause harm. So whatever Anthea was suffering from was likely only due to lack of blood. That was comforting.

"What use could it have been though? Why build something like this?"

"It was commissioned when I was quite young, to hold a phoenix that had a suicide wish. It kept flying into burning buildings but would come out fine, people started to wonder what was going on."

"What happened to the Phoenix?"

"He refused to eat, eventually starved himself to death."

I hung up the phone, feeling depressed but reassured that Anthea would survive.

Bird? Bird? Sofia and Jasper meowed coming down the stairs.

"Shoo, not your bird," I told them, and they turned slowly, walking up the stairs as if it were their own idea and not by my order. I turned to the bat. "Don't worry, I won't let them eat you."

"And what do we have here?" Evie asked, popping in.

Betina followed, hurrying down the stairs still dressed for Yoga. "Did you find Anth—what is that!" she said with a shriek, backing away after catching sight of the bat on the bed.

"Betina are you afraid of bats?"

"Why did you bring home a bat, Fawn. Filthy things, they carry rabies!" Evie said.

"Evie, this is Anthea, a Vampire Bat. Dante's daughter."

"Call it whatever you want, but don't come crying to me when you're foaming at the mouth!" Evie said then disappeared

I looked at Betina who was still keeping a safe distance. It reminded me of the way I had acted when Drake had been injured and laying on this very bed. "She's pretty hurt but I think she'll be okay after some blood. Dante went to find some."

"Is that what he's doing at the neighbor's house?"

"Christ..."

"Well, I'm going to go shower. Yeah, have fun with all that." Betina hurried upstairs.

"Scaredy cat!" I called after her, who would have thought a Troll wouldn't like bats.

Dante returned shortly with a paper cup of blood. I nearly threw up as I looked at it sloshing around. "What the hell did you—never mind, give it here." I knew I had two choices, I could save this supernatural, or I could care that Dante had probably permanently scarred and scared a human. The human would definitely live, Anthea, maybe not. I used a dropper to feed Anthea as much of the blood

157

as she would take, which wasn't a lot, but her breathing settled after that.

"I think she'll be okay. My father said the cage is harmless except for the inability to leave it, she is likely only starved half to death. Travis probably didn't even try to feed her blood." I tried to sound more than hopeful as I said it and Dante raised an eyebrow. "Yeah, I guess its one of his."

"Thank you, Fawn. I hope you don't mind her convalescing here for a couple days."

"Certainly, she's welcome as long as she needs."

"And me?" he asked quietly, closing the space between us.

I caught my breath. He was so close, his body warm, his eyes smoldering and his lips, I remember those lips. I couldn't take my eyes off of them as they slid into a smile. A noise upstairs pulled me out of my trance, and I hurried away without a word. I wasn't sure if I wanted him to stay or leave, honestly, and that scared me.

Drake and Zin were in the living room, sitting close on the couch and I couldn't help but smile at the loving picture they made. They were holding hands and Zin had her head on Drake's shoulder. There was a bit of sadness in the air, and I wondered if she knew he was going to have to leave. Pumpkin was on Drake's lap purring happily. It made me miss Logan's gentle touches. I couldn't help but wonder what he would be like when he returned. Would he be ready to make up, or would he have decided that it wasn't worth the trouble?

How dare he! I was pissed all over as if he'd decided just such a thing.

"Whoa, what's with that face?" Zin asked, dragging me out of my thoughts.

"Your brother is an asshole."

"Yep," they said in unison, and I laughed because I could have been talking about either one of their brothers, maybe I *was* talking about them both.

"I think I need to go to bed. Anthea looks like she'll be fine, she was only starved for blood I believe."

"Wonderful!" Drake said. "So will Dante be leaving soon?"

"She needs some time to fully recover." I didn't really want to address the Dante factor, but it would stand to reason that as long as Anthea was here recovering, Dante would be staying as well.

"Well, we will let you rest then. Is Logan returning soon?" Drake asked carefully.

"Should be here by morning, Kyle got away, ran North."

Drake's eyes clouded and he didn't meet my gaze. "Perhaps we should stay until he arrives or as close as we can anyway."

"I can take care of myself," I grumbled, I had resisted that handsome devil downstairs so far. I could make it through one more exhausting night.

"Of course you can!" Zin said brightly, kissing my cheek goodbye and dragging Drake out the door.

"What's he so worried about?" Evie asked, popping in.

"He thinks Dante is bad news."

"The only bad news I've heard recently is the dead fish washing up on the shore tonight, apparently its pretty weird."

"Okay Evie, goodnight." I walked upstairs; my mind full of too much. Dante's passion, Logan's dumb masculinity, Anthea's health, and my own exhausted body. I walked into my bathroom ready to wash my face and crawl into bed to sleep for hopefully an entire day, then I froze. Fish! Dead fish! "Evie!"

"What are you yelling about?"

"What did you say about dead fish?" I asked frantically.

"Oh, now you care about what I have to say?"

"Evie..." I ground out between clenched teeth. "Please tell me what you saw on the news about the fish."

"Well," she began, and I braced myself, knowing this was going to be a long story. "I was watching this cutie talking about the fishing industry the other day and he was telling all about how great they were doing lately. Such big catches, really lucky and unusual for this time of year too. Well same cutie tonight was talking about how there was a huge dump of dead fish on the shore when the tide went out, super strange. If someone doesn't clean it up it's going to be a real stink too. They think it might be pollution! Can you imagine?"

"In fact, I can, thank you Evie." I dropped onto my bed and let my thoughts swirl. The ocean was dying, I had to get the stone back in as soon as possible. But where were Bay and Eldoris? It didn't look like sleep was in my near future.

Chapter 15

"What do you mean you need a boat?" Betina asked around a spoonful of ice cream. She was sitting on the couch watching tv.

"There's something majorly wrong with the ocean."

"Right, so you got the stone thingie, right?"

"Right, but now it's got to go back in."

Betina looked at me and raised an eyebrow as she took another slow bite. "So you want me to call Tony, who I barely know but am totally into, so that we can borrow a boat and shove out into the middle of the sound in the middle of the night and drop some dumb stone into the ocean?"

"Basically."

"That's embarrassing."

"Betina if you don't do it I will call Chase and then you won't be invited," I warned.

"Okay!" Betina groaned.

I smiled and called Annabel; I couldn't do this without her.

Two hours later we were on one of the boats Tony had at his shop for a tune up and headed out into the sound. It was a roomy speedboat with just me, Annabel, Betina and Tony along for the ride. Betina had woken Tony up when she'd called, and I could tell when we got there that he'd thought she was joking and that it was really a booty call she'd been after. He answered the shop door in a pair of low-slung jeans and nothing else. His thick black hair was slicked back, and his eyes were droopy, sort of sleepy sexy is what he must have been going for. He was a Warlock, new to town, but Chase trusted him enough to introduce him to Betina, so hopefully that meant he was really trustworthy.

"Betina, baby," he drawled, "I'm so glad you—" He stopped when he noticed she wasn't alone. For a moment a new hope flashed into his eyes, but it quickly faded when he noticed my scowl. We were not there for a group booty call.

"Like I said, we really need a boat," Betina said with obvious embarrassment.

"Oh... a boat, yeah sure you said it was some kind of real serious life and death situation? Because I could really get in trouble."

"Hi, I'm Fawn Malero, perhaps you've heard of me?" I said with confidence, hoping it would carry enough weight to get him to do what we needed.

"Oh yeah, sure. Malero. Okay let me get dressed, I'll meet you guys on the dock."

"He seems nice," I said as we walked the short distance to the docks.

"He's hot!" Annabel added, jabbing an elbow into Betina's side. "And he's into you for sure!"

"Yeah, hopefully the *famous* Fawn Malero didn't just kill any chance I have of dating him."

Annabel laughed, "What was that '*you've heard of me*,' shit?"

"Well, at some point I have to make a name for myself. Why not assume I already have?"

"Its working so far," Annabel said brightly, Betina just grumbled.

Once we were out in the boat we all became very focused, this was a serious mission, and it really was life and death. I let Annabel direct Tony, she didn't have a clear idea of where to go but she'd contacted her father and got his best advice. It took over an hour to get to where we thought we needed to be.

"So are you ladies going to tell me what this is all about?" Tony cut the engine and looked at us.

It was dark except for the moonlight reflecting up off the water, but I could tell he wasn't going to be satisfied with half answers. My instinct was still to say no, but we couldn't exactly keep him hidden from this. Could we? "We need to return something to its rightful place."

Annabel stripped down to an itsy-bitsy black bikini and Tony stared, thoroughly distracted. Betina jabbed his side with her elbow and he turned to her with a sheepish smile. "Well, uh I guess I should have grabbed some towels."

I sat on the back of the boat with Annabel and stared down into the inky blackness of the water at night. "Are you sure you can do this?"

"No, but we don't really have a choice now do we? Apparently my great-grandmother was a Siren, so let's hope I have some of her abilities." Annabel held up the stone and stared at it for a moment then put the chain around her neck. "I am hoping this will allow me to be underwater for an extended period. I will go down as far as feel's safe, and I will call out, then I will come back up and we wait."

I was nervous, but our only other option was to drop the damn thing in and watch it sink and hope for the best. I had a feeling there might be more to it than that and I certainly didn't want to be responsible for it finding its way into the wrong hands again. "Don't be long."

Annabel gave me a wink and slid into the freezing water without a flinch. As soon as the stone hit the water's surface there was a blue flash that rippled like a sound wave through the water in all directions. If Annabel's voice didn't call every supernatural in the area to our boat, that certainly would.

"Woah, what the hell was that?" Tony asked, breaking the silence.

"That was very old magic," I said, a little breathless.

No one spoke but we all stared into the water, waiting. There was a pinpoint of light that I knew must be Annabel and it looked like a star in the night sky, so bright but millions of miles away. I worried

166

for my friend more than I worried our plan wouldn't work, and I don't think I took a full breath again until her head popped up out of the water. She was gasping as I helped her into the boat. She sat on the floor, and I could tell she'd stayed as long as she could down there, her lips were blue and she was shivering. Tony wrapped his coat around her and even gave her his t-shirt to use as a towel. I bent close and rubbed her legs and feet, trying to warm them. Her teeth chattered but she smiled.

"They're coming," she managed while shivering.

Tony rubbed his hands together, opened them and blew a blast of warm air at us. Annabel relaxed immediately.

"Nice trick!" Betina said, squeezing his arm and he puffed up his chest a little, smiling at her. They would be a cute couple I decided.

"How do you know it worked?" I asked even though I was positive it would too, we all saw and felt the magic ripple out.

"After the initial pulse, I went down real deep and started calling. I called for Bay and Eldoris, then I called for Mermaids and Sirens. I got an answering call from a Siren. The others, I could feel their magic pulsing out, trying to decide what I was and whether or not it was safe."

"I wish we had the same reassurance." I suddenly wondered about the chances of being overtaken and drowned out here by a mob of angry ocean supernaturals. It was too late to second guess our plan, the water around the boat started to ripple. Three red heads popped up near the back, silver eyes blinked at us from just above the water. "Mermaids," I whispered.

"Welcome!" Annabel said, but they didn't come any farther out of the water.

A red tentacle slapped over the side of the boat and hefted an octopus body onto the boat which then shifted into Eldoris. I hugged her, naked and wet, thrilled to see her again, alive, and seemingly well. "Eldoris! I am so glad you're okay, I was so worried when you never returned."

"I was too weak to shift again." Eldoris turned to the three floating heads. "It's okay ladies, this is who I was telling you about."

They floated up and moved to the back of the boat holding their upper bodies out of the water, their tails flipping up behind them. I was delighted to see that their scales covered everything from the chest down, finally an ocean supernatural who wasn't presenting themselves to me nude. They looked like triplets, long red hair, silver eyes, and flawless skin that held a greenish tone. Their lips were black and when they smiled their white teeth looked sharp and intimidating.

"You are holding Poseidon's power," they said in unison, reminding me of a scary movie. These were definitely not storybook mermaids.

"We are, and we want to make sure its returned to its rightful place and kept safe," I assured them and wished I'd brought my stun gun or at least my pepper spray. A splash near the front of the boat made me jump and turn, another splash and I recognized Bay in her seal suit making her way to us.

168

"Bay!" I called happily and the next time the seal broke through the water it barked a greeting. She jumped into the boat and quickly slid out of her skin. I heard Tony gag and tried not to laugh. It *was* a very disgusting thing to witness, especially the first time.

"Fawn, I am so grateful to see you again! And the stone, I can feel it." Bay walked to Annabel and reached out as if she were going to touch it but then stepped back. "Wow."

"We are only missing the—" I stopped, frozen by the most beautiful sound I'd ever heard. Like the sprinkling of a fine mist, it hit me gently but unmistakably and filled me with desire. My body melted and my mind focused in on the sound as it wrapped around me. I leaned over the side of the boat unaware of anything but the sound, then a face, the most beautiful face I'd ever seen. His eyes were deep blue pools and his blonde hair floated around him like a halo. I could tell he was tan, and muscled, and nude! His finger beckoned me in and I wanted nothing more than to be wrapped in his embrace. He smiled, his pink lips revealing a mouth full of perfect white teeth. "Yes," I whispered and leaned further over.

"Grab her!" I heard someone yell and then I felt strong arms yank me back. I shook my head and realized my hair was wet, my shirt soaked, and I was gasping for air but still could hear the song, the yearning song, I needed to follow it. I fought against the arms, clawing and scratching.

"Let me have him! He needs me!"

"Damnit Jason turn that shit off! She is here to help us!"

"Tony do something!"

"I can't do a spell while I'm holding her down!"

"Annabel!"

"Move out of the way."

Someone shoved something in my mouth that tasted like dirt and fish. I gagged and spit, but it was shoved back in. Annabel was in my face holding a hand over my mouth and glaring into my eyes. "Swallow damnit!"

I bit her, she screamed, and I saw and tasted blood. That's what finally brought me back to reality. There was a supernatural, a friend of mine who I loved dearly who was hurt. I had to fix this. I swallowed whatever horrible crap was in my mouth and didn't move. I waited and felt the power of whatever it had been, start to work. My mind cleared and I couldn't hear the sweet song anymore.

"What the hell happened?"

"You just experienced the full power of a Siren," Annabel explained.

"Fuck," I breathed, exhausted.

"Yeah... Jason was worried this was a trick, so he came up guns blazing," Eldoris explained apologetically. "I should have prepared you. The seaweed will keep him from working his magic on you again any time soon."

"That didn't taste like seaweed."

"Well it isn't the kind humans normally eat."

I frowned, wondering if I was in for food poisoning. I stood up slowly, Tony let me go but stayed close. I turned to him and smiled. "Thanks for keeping my head above water."

"You didn't make it easy." He winked at me.

I stepped carefully to the edge of the boat, Jason couldn't be as gorgeous as I'd thought, I was just under some kind of spell, right? I peeked carefully over. He was floating on his back, unashamed of his nakedness and he was definitely just as gorgeous, like a Greek god floating in a black pool and without any magical help I wanted to jump on top of him and ride the tide. He smiled brightly and winked as if he were reading my mind. I bit my lip, I would have to ask Annabel later if Sirens were known for mind reading skills, that would be embarrassing.

"Jason, thanks for joining us."

"My pleasure," he said and even his talking voice was silky smooth and washed over me like a gentle caress.

I stepped back before I did something embarrassing, like jump in. I looked at the expectant faces around me, a Selkie, an Octopus Shifter, three Mermaids, a Siren, a Warlock, a Troll and a half Elf-half Witch. They were all waiting for me to start. It felt so ceremonious and real I almost started with *We are gathered here today...*

"We want to return Poseidon's stone to its rightful place and be sure it doesn't end up in the wrong hands ever again." There was a murmur of agreement. "Is there such a place already picked?"

"There's a cave where it will be safe," Eldoris said.

"And all are in agreement?" I looked around, there was not one supernatural here that I wanted to piss off unintentionally. There were all nods of agreement. "Great, and who will be taking the stone?"

"I'm here to provide my services as guardian of the stone," Jason said, and looked at me intensely. "And any other services that might be needed."

The Mermaids giggled and I bit my lip, forcing myself to turn to Annabel. Her eyes were soft, and she was smiling at Jason. "Perhaps you should accompany Jason to the stone's final resting place?" I suggested.

Annabel's eyes widened then relaxed back to her normal not caring. "I suppose I should see this to its end." She gave me a quick squeeze and slipped into the water. "I'll find my way home."

Eldoris gave me a kiss on the cheek. "Thank you, Fawn you are amazing!"

"Just doing my job."

"You know its more than that," Bay added. "I hope to see you again sometime."

"Yes, you are both welcome any time at my house when you want to play at land lover for a time."

They both laughed. Eldoris jumped, shifted midair, and splashed into the water in octopus form. Bay slipped back into her seal skin and flopped back into the water a little less gracefully. The Mermaids said *thank you* in unison and pushed away from the boat. Jason grabbed Annabel's hand and gave me a wink before pushing off. "I'm sure we will see each other again," he called before slipping under the water with Annabel.

"I hope she's safe," I whispered as they disappeared in the inky blackness.

"She knows what she's doing," Betina reassured me.

I stared into the water until the light from the stone disappeared. Then we headed back to the dock. If it wasn't for Tony's ability to keep us surrounded by a pocket of warm air, I think I would have froze to death. My hair and shirt were soaked, I can't believe I almost drowned myself because of lust. I guess the stories of Siren's luring sailors to their doom was quite plausible.

As we docked, the sun was coming up and I knew I was going to have to face Logan soon. In the short time he'd been gone I'd almost let Dante have his way with me, without any outside magical influence, and almost thrown myself into the underwater arms of Jason, of course that one wasn't entirely my fault. What was wrong with me? I was acting like a horny teenager, and I hadn't even been this horny when I *was* a teenager!

"Hey, thanks again, Tony. I really appreciate you taking that risk and getting us out there tonight."

"My pleasure, I am always willing to help a lovely lady, and that was fucking cool!"

I walked ahead to the car, wanting to give Betina and Tony a moment alone. When she got in the passenger seat her cheeks were still red and she was vibrating with happiness.

"He kissed me!"

"Wow! That's great, he seems like a really nice guy."

"He does, doesn't he," she smiled and wiggled in her seat.

I hoped he didn't break her heart; they were both so young.

"Do you think Logan's back yet?"

I frowned as I drove. "I think he must be back by now, though I don't know if he'll be waiting for us at the house."

"Of course he will, he is so totally into you and you guys have been apart for days! I am sure he's ready to jump your bones again."

"Betina!"

"Well, do you think I don't know what goes on between you two?"

My face flushed, "Well let's just hope he doesn't think I smell like fish."

"Are you going to tell him that you almost threw yourself into the arms of a devilishly handsome Siren?"

"Definitely not."

"Because he might try to kill Jason?"

"Exactly."

Betina seemed to accept that answer and sat quietly for a moment. "What about Dante?"

I stiffened. "What about Dante?"

"Oh, don't play that with me! I know he's got the hots for you and he's damn sexy, I know you've noticed that too."

"I am dating Logan."

"Right... so that means you're dead inside to the charms of anyone else."

"When did you become the expert on romance?"

"I read a lot."

We sat in silence the rest of the way home and when I saw Logan's truck out front I relaxed. My heart started pounding and I smiled. Yeah, I was definitely picking the right guy.

"Why didn't you wait for me?" Logan demanded from the front porch.

"Hey! Glad you're back!" Betina slapped his back and walked past him into the house. "I'm going to bed, goodnight."

I stopped at the bottom of the steps and stared up at Logan. He was standing with hands on hips and a bit of a glare on his face. "You should have waited till I could go with you."

"Logan I—" I wanted to rant and yell and fight about how I could do anything without him and didn't need him and he would just have to deal with that. But right now I didn't have the energy and if I was really thinking about it, I knew he was coming from a place of fear, not anger. "I am fine, but I am tired, and I missed you. Take me to bed?"

He growled, grabbed me, and pulled me in for a fierce kiss full of longing. He scooped me up in his arms and carried me inside and up to bed. I had no intention of getting out of bed before noon.

Chapter 16

I woke slowly, stretching languidly and cuddling up to the warm body next to me. I was kind of surprised Logan was still in bed, he wasn't usually a languisher. He leaned down and kissed the spray of freckles across the bridge of my nose. It was a favorite spot for him to put his lips. My face heated thinking of his other favorite spots.

"I love to see you blush in the morning, are you reliving our early morning activities?"

"I might be," I giggled and reached up to pull him in for a proper kiss. He sighed and pulled back giving me a stern look. "We have to get up don't we?" I whined.

"Yes, but you're not making it easy. I have to talk to Tony, I want to get a read on him myself, even if you and Chase think he's a good guy."

"Not a bad idea."

His face turned serious, and I filled with worry. "We need to talk about who's in the basement."

"Dante?"

"No, Anthea."

"Oh, is she alright?" I shot up in bed, kicking myself for not checking on her when I returned last night, what if she needed medical attention.

"Relax, she's fine. I checked in on them last night when I was waiting for you to get home."

I sat back filled with relief. "Okay, good."

"But there's something you need to know." His voice was serious and full of caution, it wasn't like him to talk this way, especially not in bed.

"Logan, you're scaring me." My heart was beating a million miles an hour and my body was heating, but none of it was from the usual passion, this was all fear and loathing. I could feel a similar reaction rolling off of Logan's body, whatever this was, it was bad.

"Anthea came here to find Drake, to give him a message about returning to his father."

"Yes, I was hoping it wouldn't come to that, but there's nothing we can do about it." I had a sudden crazy thought, had Logan been asked to bargain me for his friend's freedom? Was I about to be sold to Dante for a night of unimaginable pleasure!

"Well, that's not the only reason she was here."

"Right, something about a fiancé."

"Right." Logan took a deep breath and closed his eyes. "That would be me."

I couldn't breathe, I couldn't move, and I couldn't speak. Logan was engaged! To Anthea!

Anger filled me and I was ready to explode so I didn't cry. "What the hell is wrong with you! What are you doing with me if you're engaged to someone else?"

"It was years ago, then we fought and I left, we haven't talked to each other in ten years. That's not a real engagement."

"Then why is she here looking for her fucking fiancé?" I jumped out of the bed and stalked to the bathroom slamming the door shut and sliding down it. I was barely holding back the tears. I did *not* want him to hear me cry.

"Fawn," Logan whispered through the door. "Fawn. I will talk to her as soon as she is awake, I have no desire to marry her, she hasn't crossed my mind in years, and I want—I want to be with you. Just you."

The tears were running down my face and I didn't want him to know, he didn't deserve my tears. I didn't want him to know so I said nothing.

"Damnit Fawn, talk to me!"

Evie appeared in the bathroom. "Do you want me to call the police?"

"No," I whispered.

"Evie open the door!" Logan demanded.

"He sounds very angry."

"He is engaged to that bat downstairs."

Evie's eyes widened and then turned to slits, she disappeared. "Asshole!" I heard her say from the other side of the door. "How dare you treat sweet Fawn this way!" Her defense of me made me smile.

"What's all the yelling?" Betina said from the bedroom.

179

Great now everyone was here.

"Logan's engaged to the twit downstairs," Evie said angrily, and I could imagine she was standing with her hands on hips.

"What! What the hell is wrong with you, Logan?"

"Its complicated," he growled, and I wondered how close he was to shifting and busting through my wall.

"So complicated that Fawn is locked in the bathroom crying!" Evie accused.

"Perhaps you should go," Betina said quietly.

Logan growled deep. "Maybe you should mind your own business, Troll!"

I was about to open the door to keep him from attacking anyone, I could smell rotten milk and fish, Betina was scared.

"Fawn, I am going to go for a walk, and I am going to go talk to Tony, then I will be back and we *will* talk about this." I heard his retreating foot stomps and the front door slam. Then I opened the bathroom door and let Betina give me a comforting hug.

"Why is he going to talk to Tony?"

I rolled my eyes at her selfish concern. "He wants to make sure the guy is good enough for you."

"Awe, that's so sweet."

I glared at her.

"Sorry," she shrugged.

"So, what's with all this? Logan is engaged?"

"Yeah, apparently he's the fiancé that Anthea had come here looking for."

"No shit!" Betina's mouth was wide.

"Yeah... so I feel like a complete idiot."

"You shouldn't, he lied to you, how were you supposed to know he was in love with someone else?"

I sighed, "He says he broke it off ten years ago after they got in a fight."

Betina looked confused. "So then what's the problem?"

"Why would she be here if she didn't think they were still engaged, and why didn't he tell me? He should have told me as soon as Drake showed up. I deserved to know his possible future father-in-law was in my basement!"

"Yes, he should have told you."

I laid on my bed trying to decide if I was madder at his betrayal or scared, he was going to leave me for a Vampire bat. "I'm going to take a shower."

The hot water did a lot to calm me and by the time I was dressed I knew I needed all the information and the best place to get it was from Anthea. I walked downstairs and found Dante sitting in a chair smiling as I descended.

"I heard quite the commotion; I suppose you know that Logan is engaged to my daughter." His voice was emotionless, and I appreciated that he wasn't gloating or trying to take advantage of my weakened emotional state.

"I do," I said simply and walked to the table. Anthea was out of bat form, but she was still sleeping. She was absolutely beautiful, and I wanted to cry all over again. Flawless white skin, deep red lips that were perfectly pouty. She was tall and very thin. Dante had covered her in a blanket, and I made a mental note to get some clothes for her. "She looks much better."

"Yes, I expect she'll wake soon. I will need to get more blood as soon as the sun goes down."

"Does she love him?"

He sighed heavily. "No, she came to officially break up with him. In her mind their ten-year fight hadn't ended the relationship even though she'd been entirely unfaithful the whole time. She is now enamored with a Vampire who she wants to marry. She feels obligated to face Logan and break their engagement first."

This was a huge relief, it didn't take away the hurt, but at least I wasn't going to have to fight a Vampire for Logan's hand, I was sure to lose a duel like that. "Well, that's good. Would you like me to take a look at her?"

"Thank you but I am confident she just needs rest and blood."

"I will get her something she can wear when she wakes up and I will have Logan pick up some blood." I knew he could run by Lila's bar and grab some, saving the life of my neighbors.

"Thank you, your kindness in the face of the situation is invaluable. I would love to thank you properly."

He came up behind me and ran his hands up and down my arms. I felt his lips press gently against my neck and I shivered. It would be so easy to let him have his way with me, to blame my anger at Logan for my own betrayal, but I couldn't. If I had any hope of repairing things with Logan, which I wasn't completely sure I wanted to do, I had to walk away from Dante.

I turned and stepped away, looking into his eyes that were fired up with desire. "You could talk to your father about allowing Drake to stay here, he's been intricate to my investigations on multiple occasions."

Dante looked disappointed but nodded. "I will put in the recommendation. I have called my brother Ezra, he will arrive tonight and as long as Anthea is well enough, we will be leaving." He stepped forward and touched my chin lightly. "But I will return any time, Fawn, any time you want me." His voice was gruff, and I turned to run before I could betray myself.

I gathered some clothing for Anthea and sent them down with Betina, then messaged Logan to go by the bar and get blood for Anthea. The sooner she was healthy, the sooner she would be out of our lives. I decided not to tell him yet what Dante had said, he deserved a little time worrying about things.

He returned with blood, and flowers. He had the biggest puppy dog sad eyes, and he was facing me, Evie, and Betina, all with arms across our chests, glaring. "You think flowers are going to make me forgive you?"

"These are for Betina," he said handing her a bouquet of wildflowers. "I met Tony and he seems really nice, and I am sorry I yelled at you."

"Forgiven," she said and gave him a quick kiss.

"And for Evie," he handed her an autographed picture of a local hottie news reporter who just happened to be a Werewolf. I recognized it from Lila's bar, she was going to be pissed when she saw it was missing.

"Forgiven!" Evie said. "Hang it there, where I can stare at it." She pointed to a space of wall near the bathroom, and I rolled my eyes. I was going to have to see that damn picture for the rest of my life no doubt.

"Betina, can you run this blood downstairs," Logan handed her a paper bag.

"For your fiancé," she said with disgust.

"For Fawn's patient," he said and turned to me. "For you." He held out his hand and in his palm was a tiny silver chain with a small silver wolf charm. He put it around my neck and stepped back, admiring it. "You know you're the only female I want."

I raised an eyebrow and inspected the gift; its eyes were small brown stones and in a way it resembled Logan. "Its beautiful."

"I am going to break things off, officially, just as soon as Anthea is awake. I already told Dante I have no intention of ever marrying his daughter the first time I met with him in the basement. I told him I would do whatever necessary to help find her, but I would not be obligated to marry her."

I looked at Logan and took pity. "Dante told me that she is in love with a Vampire and came here to break the engagement."

Logan's eyes lit up, then he glared. "You could have told me that! Or he could have…"

"Do you really think you deserved to not feel bad?" I huffed.

He growled and pulled me close, crushing me just the right amount, then pressed his lips to mine. "I guess I deserved it," he said after he'd kissed me breathless, and my mind had melted. He smiled down at me very satisfied with himself and what he could do to me. "But it will be good for us to talk and end the engagement for good."

"She's awake," Betina said, startling us both.

Logan let me go but only enough so that I could turn and look at Betina, his arm was around my shoulder, keeping me close. "That's good I suppose."

"Go talk to her, no reason to wait." I tried to sound matter of fact, but my voice hitched a little with emotions I was trying very hard to hold back.

"Yes, then we need to talk about Mr. S."

I got excited. "Did he respond?"

"He did."

"Well! What did he say?"

"He said he has a bottle of very old perfume that will help me win over any lady."

I gasped. "Aphrodite's perfume?"

"I think so, though he didn't say that's what it was."

"So, what now?"

"Now we need to respond, something that won't make him suspicious but gets him back here to give it to us, then we apprehend him."

"Sounds easy enough, any ideas?"

"I think we try to get him to meet us somewhere private."

185

"Here in Seattle?" That didn't seem likely to me, he's too smart to not be suspicious.

"No, I'm thinking we say we're from somewhere else. I have a cousin in Coeur d'Alene, Idaho. I think we could go there for a couple days and set up a meeting." Logan leaned in close. "It would be a nice little getaway, maybe we could have some time alone. Your house has been pretty crowded lately."

I couldn't agree more with that statement. Even if Dante and Anthea left tonight, Logan and I needed some time to connect, a five-hour drive would be good for that.

Logan grimaced. "I'll give Carine a call, we can leave tonight. But first, I'll talk to Anthea."

I tried to keep myself busy while he was downstairs, I started to clean the kitchen but caught my reflection in the window. The small wolf charm with its deep brown eyes seemed to be looking up at me, mouth open a bit. Had it always looked like that? I took it off and looked closer. Its mouth was closed and it was looking straight ahead. "What the hell?" I put it back on and again it seemed to be looking at me.

"It's charmed to watch you," Logan said, coming up behind me. "Its a link to me. Inside it is a lock of my fur and I can feel you as long as you wear it. I wouldn't be able to lose you if you ran to the other side of the world unless you took it off." He smiled shyly. "I hope you won't."

I was slightly worried this was some kind of Werewolf engagement ring but didn't want to ask. "I love it Logan, and as long as it isn't spying on me, but just some kind of locator spell, I can handle that."

"No spying," he laughed. "Although maybe I should be worried about what you're up to when I'm gone, you smell a little like Dante today…"

I nearly choked, fumbling for a reason. "I—I was downstairs to check on Anthea I—"

"I don't own you, Fawn. I don't want to," he gritted out and I very much doubted that statement. "You're free to leave me any time."

I smiled at his obvious discomfort and how hard he was trying to be reasonable. "Did you break off your engagement?"

"Yes, she was very happy to be done with me. I am almost hurt," he joked.

I wrapped my arms around his neck. "I don't want anyone else, Logan. I might even love you."

He smiled and his eyes flashed with passion. "I might even love you too, Fawn." He scooped me up in his arms then and hurried up the stairs growling passionately. Very quickly I was only wearing the necklace.

Chapter 17

Logan made arrangements with his cousin and left to pack for a quick trip. I was anxious to get out of the house and away from Dante and Anthea. I think he was too. Betina was at the yoga studio so I called her and told her she'd have the house to herself, which meant she should call Annabel or Chase to stay with her and the other guests would be leaving that night. I was glad I knew my studio would be fine without me, I could really try to enjoy my time away, even if it was still official P.I. business.

"So, you forgave Logan?" Evie asked, popping in while I was stepping out of the shower. She was wearing a sweater today and slacks, she rarely dressed so appropriately for the weather.

"Are you going out today?" I asked, changing the subject.

"Oh you know me, just a homebody. I'll let you do all the running around."

The way she said *running around* seemed chastising. "I should probably *run* downstairs and tell Dante I will be leaving for a few days, tell him my goodbyes now." Meet the infamous Anthea officially.

I grabbed a couple bags of blood stashed in the fridge and walked downstairs. Dante was sitting silently in a corner and on the bed, Anthea was sleeping again.

"I came to check on her, but it seems she is well." I threw the bags at him and he caught them with one hand, never losing eye contact.

"It's cold."

"Sorry," I said with a raised eyebrow. "I'm heading out of town for a few days."

He stood then and crossed the room. "With Logan?"

"Yes."

Dante reached out and ran a finger along my cheek, sending shivers down my spine. "Sweet Fawn, I am so disappointed in your denial of both our pleasure."

"So full of yourself," I managed a little breathlessly.

"I'm patient," he said, stepping back. "I will wait to collect on the promise of your kisses."

He moved back to his seat and ripped seductively into the bag of blood. Why did I find this scene so enticing! What the hell was wrong with me? I turned and ran before I could do or say anything to encourage him. His laughter followed me.

I was packed and ready when Logan returned.

"So, what's your cousin like?" I asked as we drove through the heavy Seattle traffic. As the distance between me and Dante lengthened, I felt more and more sure that he had been using some kind of power to entice me, I am probably incredibly lucky it didn't work.

Logan smiled, "Carine is very rambunctious."

"What the hell is that supposed to mean?"

"You'll love her, she's very sweet."

I decided my questions would get me nowhere, so I stopped and just enjoyed the ride. The silence was comfortable and cathartic, we needed to connect after these last few days of insanity, but sometimes comfortable silence did more than talking could.

Five hours later we were pulling into the little city just as the sun was starting to descend past the horizon. There was a beautiful orange and pink sunset behind us, and I felt super girly, wanting to hold Logan's hand and squeal about it. I resisted though.

I also couldn't wait to get out of the truck, and I looked around anxiously as Logan pulled off of the freeway and drove through the town. "So where does your cousin live? Is she far from town?" A lot of Werewolves chose to live in places that were somewhat secluded and often they backed up to some kind of wooded area.

"Carine likes to swim, so she has a place near the lake."

"Oh how fun, too bad its too cold to enjoy." Logan weaved through neighborhood streets and by tiny houses I prayed he wasn't going to stop at, this would not be better than my house if we were stuck in some one bedroom with his cousin. He kept going though and soon the houses started to get bigger. He slowed when we came to what could only be described as a castle! Complete with gargoyles on the front porch! "No!" I said, more than a little impressed.

"Yep, it'll make sense when you meet Jax."

"Her husband?"

"Her wife."

"Oh!" I wondered why Logan was being so secretive, I had nothing against anyone's choice in love. I was the last one who should be judgmental about choices in love. Logan pulled around the back, through an alley that passed behind the house and pulled to a stop in front of a set of garage doors. I couldn't see anything through the windows and wondered at what kind of fancy cars they might have in there, then I realized all the windows of the house were pretty dark, maybe they weren't home. "Logan, are they expecting us?" I asked anxiously.

"Oh yes," he laughed. "Carine is very excited to meet you. I'm afraid her and Lila are very close, so she's heard all about you."

I could only hope I lived up to Lila's descriptions. Logan walked around the truck and opened my door then grabbed our bags out of the back. I took a moment to enjoy the lungful of fresh air, cold but fresher than Seattle air.

"Nice, isn't it?" Logan said, reading my mind, or maybe just my expression.

"It reminds me of being out at your place." Logan's house was a cabin in the mountains outside of Seattle when he wasn't sleeping in the back room of his construction company's office. Though he'd basically moved in with me before we started fighting, which had occurred when Dante had shown up. I couldn't help blaming him, he's probably been manipulating more than my libido.

"Logan!" A voice called from the back door and a small woman rushed outside, smaller than the Werewolf females I'd met before. She had long white hair pulled back in two French braids and bright blue eyes. Her skin was paler than most Werewolves I'd seen too. Then it hit me, this was Logan's mother's niece, she must be from the Alaska pack as well. They were apparently smaller and paler than the Washington pack.

"Carine!" Logan yelled back and they embraced each other. Logan lifted her off the ground in a bear hug. When he set her back down she turned to me. "This is Fawn," Logan said motioning me forward.

"Fawn!" She hurried to me then and embraced me tightly. She was definitely strong like a Werewolf. "I am so glad to see Logan settled down," she whispered in my ear and kissed my cheek that was now reddened.

"Thank you so much for letting us invade your space on such short notice."

"Of course! We love to have guests," she said brightly, and I had no doubt she meant it.

I looked around expectantly, where was this wife of hers? The most beautiful woman I had ever seen walked out of the house, she was tall, taller than Logan and she was incredibly thin, and pale, Vampire. Her eyes were a bright blue and she had long straight black hair that reached her waist. She had bright red lips that were plump and wide. When she smiled I could see all of her teeth and I was willing to bet she didn't go out in public much. She looked so foreign; she'd never pass inspection by a cautious human.

"Jax!" Logan said happily, giving the woman a wave. She stayed on the porch; it was still a little too bright out here for her but she was safe in the shadow of the house.

"Logan, I am so glad you've come, and brought your mate." Her voice was thick with an unidentifiable accent. I honestly wouldn't be surprised to hear she was from Transylvania, straight out of Dracula's coven.

She made me nervous, I stepped close to Logan and put a hand on his arm and smiled at her. "Thank you for opening your home to us, Jax."

"Family is always welcome in our home," she said simply.

I really didn't love being called Logan's mate, it sounded so archaic. Made me feel like he'd hit me over the head with a club and dragged me home to his mamma's cave. But I felt like right now was not the time to complain. I wanted Jax to think of me as family, I was sure she had a rule against eating family, hopefully.

Logan squeezed my arm reassuringly.

"Carine, you have guests!" The voice made me jump and I nearly screamed, we all turned to see a woman walking her collie through the alley, a human woman. The dog looked at Logan and yipped *Friend!* Then tried to pull his owner toward Logan. "Hey, Roxie! What's the matter with you?" She looked at us apologetically, trying to hold it still.

"Yes, family from Seattle," Carine said. I glanced behind us and noticed Jax was nowhere to be found.

"Well, welcome to our beautiful city." The woman had to practically drag the dog away. I poked Logan with my elbow, and he gave a growl so quiet I knew the woman wouldn't pick it up, but the dog did and hurried to obey Logan's command, walking nicely now beside it's owner.

"You have quite the effect on dogs," Carine said, laughing at Logan.

"Don't you?" I asked before I could stop and think if it would be a rude question.

"Not as much, I am not quite so dominant a personality as Logan, I guess. They like me but they don't want to follow my every command like they do when Logan's around."

"I've noticed that about him, I have two dogs at home who couldn't care less about me since he's come sniffing around."

Carine laughed, Logan growled, and we all walked to the house. The inside was decorated in an expectedly goth style. Jax met us just inside the door, then they gave a tour of the main floor. Mud room, kitchen, living area and two bathrooms on this floor as well as a double car garage. "Master bedroom and laundry," Carine said motioning to a door under the stairs that must have led to the basement. Then we followed them up. As we went, the house was suddenly opened up, all the blinds lifted and although the glass was all slightly tinted, it was comforting to see a bit of the outside where night had fallen.

"Automatic window shades, very high tech," Logan said.

"It is a luxury I require," Jax said simply.

The upper floor held two suites that each included a large bedroom and bathroom as well as a small sitting area. We were given the largest of them and I was happy it was decorated a bit brighter than the rest of the house. Grey and blue that reminded me of a stormy morning on the shore. "Your home is beautiful."

"Thank you, Jax is the interior decorator." Carine beamed at Jax and lifted up on tiptoes, which still wasn't enough, Jax had to lean down, and they kissed sweetly. Carine turned back to us. "We are hosting a little get together in your honor tonight, I hope you feel up to it! The drive wasn't too terrible?"

"The drive was fine," Logan said for both of us. "We might just rest here a bit before the guests arrive, if there's time?"

"Certainly! We will be down in the kitchen if you need anything." Carine and Jax left quickly, and Logan closed the door behind them.

"I've been sniffing around your place, huh?" Logan growled playfully and crouched low, stalking.

I giggled and put the large bed between us. "What would you call it?" My body was heating, my heart pumping, I knew that look in Logan's eyes. He had one thing on his mind and my body was responding quickly.

"I would say you've had a Vampire sniffing around recently and I have been protecting my territory," he said jumping onto the bed and pulling me off the floor quickly. He fell back holding me gently.

"Is that what I am? Your territory? Or is it your mate?" I teased.

He flipped me onto my back and started to undress me. "Whatever you want to call it, as long as you don't try to stop me." He slipped his hands between us, and I arched my back. I had no intention of stopping him.

Chapter 18

After we showered and dressed, I was feeling nervous about meeting a bunch of new supernaturals. Logan wasn't any help; he didn't know who they might have invited from local packs. There was a rather large Werewolf pack farther north and a large Vampire coven in the neighboring city of Spokane, but the supernaturals in Coeur d'Alene were more elusive, less organized.

"I know there are a lot of ghosts down near the old fort grounds, if you miss Evie."

I rolled my eyes. "I don't think I would miss Evie in anything less than a three-month vacation. Haven't you been here before, don't you know their friends?"

"The last time I was here was with my parents, we didn't have a party."

I frowned; this was unnerving. I'd put on jeans and a tight black sweater with a plunging neckline. I wrapped a grey and red scarf around my neck and hoped this was appropriate for whatever kind of party we were attending. Logan wore jeans and a t-shirt; he didn't care and he looked amazing.

"Try not to look so nervous, Fawn."

"Right," I grumbled. We made our way downstairs just as guests were starting to arrive. Carine had set out trays of snacks and there were bottles of wine on the kitchen table ready to be opened. The first guests looked perfectly human. A man and woman of average height and athletic builds. Both with shaggy brown hair and deep dark brown eyes. They moved with a kind of heavy gait that seemed like it should come with a much larger heavier frame. Carine walked them over to us.

"Logan, Fawn these are some great local friends of ours. The first supernaturals we met in the area actually. John and Tara, they are Bigfoot Shifters."

I am sure my face showed disbelief on a level that was ridiculous given the fact that I had recently met a very sweet Octopus Shifter and was standing next to a couple Werewolves, and a Vampire, but seriously Bigfoot! Bigfoot wasn't real!

Logan pinched me. "So nice to meet you two," he said, hopefully covering my rudeness.

"Do you live near here?" I asked, recovering, and remembering my manners.

"Just down the road actually, we like to roam over the hill there, Tubbs Hill the local's call it." The woman's voice was deep, and I could now understand why they seemed to walk heavy, their mass was hidden in their human form. In the same way that Eldoris seemed so much smaller than she looked in her human form, as if her mass were less, theirs was incredibly greater. I hoped I would get an opportunity to see them in their other form, though I would never ask, that felt extremely personal and rude.

The doorbell rang then and distracted everyone. Jax let in the next guests, these creatures I recognized as a couple young female Vampires. I was thankful for the familiarity. Their names were Selene and Jean, twins actually who had driven over from Spokane to be at the party. They had matching pixie cut black hair and nose rings. They wore black lipstick and tight leather pants with black lacy tank tops. The only thing different about them was their jackets. Selene was wearing a pink leather cropped jacket and Jean wore a longer cut jean jacket. I made a mental note and prayed they didn't take them off.

The next guest was unfamiliar, but the smell told me she had come from the lake. Her hair was a soft grey color and her skin pure white. Her lips held a tint of blue and from where I stood, her eyes seemed to be the same grey as her hair. She was quite lovely, average height and very slim build. She was wearing a long white dress that flowed around her almost as if it were floating in water. "Loch ness monster?" I whispered to Logan. We were across the room pouring some wine so I was sure they wouldn't hear. He laughed.

"I would guess Lady of the Lake."

"Like King Arthur legends?"

"Yes, a Witch who has devoted herself to the spirit and magic of a lake. She lives within its shielding waters, protecting the water and shore in return she gains power from the spirit held by the water itself. She can disappear completely into the water, translucent.

Carine walked our way with the woman whose eyes swept over me curiously. "Logan, Fawn, this is Fiona."

Fiona held her hand out to me, I took it in a light grasp. She surprised me by clamping down and pulling me forward. Her hand was ice cold and her eyes flowed between grey and blue and black as she stared deeply into mine. I could feel Logan tense up behind me.

"You've touched the stone," Fiona said breathless. Her other hand slid over top mine and she brought my hand to her lips, giving it a slight kiss. She closed her eyes and sighed.

"What's going on?" Jax asked cautiously, coming up behind Fiona.

"I don't know," Carine replied.

"These hands have held Poseidon's stone; I can still feel a trace of his power. Its intoxicating." Fiona opened her eyes and smiled; she moved my hand away from her face but didn't let go. "You must tell me everything."

Fiona moved me to a corner of the room where we could sit and talk. Logan watched us go helplessly, no use being rude and telling her no. I gave him a shrug and he settled into conversation with the Bigfoot couple.

I told Fiona everything I knew about the stone, I didn't leave anything out, I couldn't, she pressed me for every detail she even thought I might have missed.

"I wish I could have seen it. Perhaps someday I will visit you in Seattle and your friend, Annabel can show me."

"Yes, of course."

"Will you come with me?"

"Sure, you come to Seattle, and I will help Annabel show you where the stone is."

"No, right now, will you come with me?"

I looked around nervously. Logan was deep in conversation with the Bigfoot Shifters and Carine was missing, probably in the kitchen preparing more food. Jax was sitting between the twins on the couch in a way that made me wonder if they had an intimate relationship. Fiona grabbed my hand and pulled me up and out of the house before anyone took any notice. She rushed through the yard, across the street, and down a short stretch of beach to the water's edge. It was cold, I didn't have a coat, and the breeze drifting off the water made me shiver. "Fiona what—"

"Touch the water with me. I just want some of that magic in my lake."

I thought she was surely nuts, but I understood what she wanted so I bent down and ran my hands through the frigid water. Nothing happened at first, other than me feeling silly. Fiona crouched beside me and put her hand in the water next to mine. "Kiss me," she said.

"I'm flattered but—"

Fiona rolled her eyes, cutting off my argument and making me feel silly. She put one hand behind my head and pulled me forward until our lips met. It wasn't an enthusiastic kiss, but it was invasive. I could feel her magic spill into my mouth and rush throughout my body like cold water. It rushed and moved, searching. It found what it was looking for in my hands and I felt it spring from my fingertips. Fiona pulled away and I looked down at my hands in the water. A glowing blue haze was wafting off of my hands and dissipating into the lake.

"Fawn, what the hell are you doing out here?" Logan's voice broke the silence.

"Sharing some of her magic," Fiona answered, holding my hands under the water until the glow stopped.

Logan moved close enough to watch the end of what was happening. "I thought perhaps Fiona was trying to lure you into her underwater lair."

I knew he was referencing the kiss he'd no doubt seen, and my face flushed a little. "I can't be tempted away from you that easy." Fiona finally let go of my hands and I stood up, surprisingly my hands felt warm, maybe it was hypothermia. Logan pulled me close, possessive.

"Tell Carine and Jax that I had to go," Fiona said and stepped into the water. Where the small waves lapped against her ankles they disappeared, her feet were gone too I realized. As she moved forward in the water everything it touched seemed to just disappear or become part of the water maybe.

We stood there watching until she was completely gone. "Trippy," Logan said, squeezing my hand. "So, was she a good kisser?"

My face flamed. "Logan, you know that—"

"Oh, don't you worry, I understand magic pretty well." We both knew she could have gotten the same result in a less intrusive manner, but nothing was quicker than the lips for pouring magic into someone else. We walked back to the house, and it was buzzing, more guests had arrived. A few more Werewolves and Vampires. "A wood nymph," I gasped. I knew it as soon as I saw her. Of course, it wasn't too hard to guess. Her clothes were made of leaves, and they were extremely skimpy. She had long red curly hair and I was sure I saw a stick or two mixed in with the locks.

"Fawn! You ran off with Fiona, is everything all right?" Carine rushed over when she noticed us.

"Oh yes, I was just helping her with something. She's decided to head back home already."

"Well, that's too bad, she can be quite the party girl. Perhaps another night. Come, meet the others."

Carine introduced us to all the newcomers, and we enjoyed a really nice evening of conversation and food. By the time we'd made it to bed I was exhausted and a little tipsy. "Did we really agree to take a stroll at dawn with the Bigfoots, Bigfeet?"

"Yes, but I'll let you sleep in. I think I want to wolf out with Carine for it anyway."

"Awesome!" I fell into bed still half dressed and I didn't care one bit. It was probably an hour till dawn, and I had no intention of waking up before noon.

Chapter 19

The room was dark when I woke up, but with the darkened windows and drawn shades there was no way of knowing what it was really like outside. I rolled over and found the bed empty, Logan must still be out running wild on the hill. I showered and dressed casually, then made my way downstairs. Logan, Carine and Jax were sitting in the kitchen. Logan and Carine were drinking coffee and I was thankful for that! I needed a cup or two.

"Good morning, love," Carine greeted, jumping up to pour me a cup.

Logan stood and gave me a quick but passionate kiss. "You slept well?"

"I did! What time is it?"

"Two in the afternoon," Carine said, handing me the cup. "You missed morning exercise and mid-morning naptime," she laughed.

"Maybe tomorrow." I sipped my coffee and looked at Logan, wondering if I could ask him about Stefan in front of everyone or not. "Do we have any... plans made for our vacation?"

"Its all right, they know why we're here. I got a message from Mr. S last night; he'll be in the area tonight and is willing to meet me."

"That's great!"

"Except he expects to meet a human guy in a public place who needs help attracting women. Even if he hadn't met me before, he would never buy that I need help meeting women."

"Full of yourself," Jax sniffed.

"Regardless of your status as god's gift to women, he knows you. Why didn't we think of that before! We need someone he's never met, preferably someone nondescript and human." I couldn't believe we hadn't thought of that before. Stefan would never get close if he saw us, and of course he wants to meet somewhere public.

"I can get the human to play pathetic male," Jax said casually. "But how do you expect to apprehend Mr. S in the process?"

"Maybe we don't." Everyone looked at me expectantly. I was fingering the wolf charm at my chest. "We obviously have to pay him, right? So, what if we put a tracing spell on the money? Then we just have to follow it to him."

"I like it, so we need a human pawn and a Witch to cast the spell," Logan looked at Carine. "Do you know a local Witch who might be willing to help?"

"Maybe, I know one, but she doesn't like me much," Carine admitted.

"Perhaps if I go with you to talk to her?" I offered.

"Couldn't hurt."

"Great, Logan you just make sure we have the cash ready and the shackles handy," I said, feeling good about taking control. Soon Carine and I were in her car and on our way to meet what she described as an old ass cranky Witch. Fun!

"So how is Jax going to manage with the whole human thing?"

Carine looked at me sternly. "Logan tells me you are pretty leery of Vampires still."

I thought about the Vampire in my basement who I wanted to jump on and see what terrifyingly intense things he had planned for me. Drake and Zin, who were two of my best friends. Jax seemed pretty okay too. But whenever I thought about their teeth, their fangs sucking blood, their tongues lapping it up. I shivered; I just didn't like it. "They're growing on me."

"Jax is... old school, she doesn't go for packaged blood and its not easy to get all the time, we have a small hospital."

"So she drains humans!"

"No! She feeds off of one or two humans who she glamours to think they are making love. No harm done; she never takes much."

"So she is going to glamour some poor human to do this for us?"

"No, that's too dangerous, Mr. S would probably notice he was off right away. The guy is completely devoted to her, he'll volunteer for the job without asking any questions at all. He's into being dominated."

"Oh... well then I guess he probably doesn't mind."

"Can you keep a secret?"

"Of course."

"Jax doesn't glamour him anymore, he is just left wondering if she is what he thinks she might be."

I gasped, "That's illegal!"

"Only if someone finds out."

"Isn't there someone who keeps the order in this city that you're afraid might find out?"

"This is kind of a free zone. The Werewolves keep order north of here and the Vampires watch over the city to the West. We don't need that here, everyone is self governing and until we prove otherwise, no one will step up to try and control anyone else."

Part of me hated that, I was a Magician, we were born to be order keepers! Of course, it wasn't really any of my business, as long as the humans were still kept in the dark. "I'm glad its working out." Was all I could think to say.

We pulled up to a tiny house a little way out of town. There was a huge garden out front and a couple cats on the porch. Typical for a Witch. "What happened to her coven?"

"Celeste lived here with her daughter for years I guess, I don't really know anything before that. She could have come from anywhere. Her daughter left eventually but she is still here. She's quite old, probably the oldest thing I've ever met."

Which also meant she was extremely powerful and potentially dangerous. We walked up to the front porch; the door opened before we reached the first step. A woman stepped out and if I were a human, I would look at this woman and think Witch. She wasn't even trying to hide it. She was short and round and she was wearing a long skirt that was a patchwork of colors and black lace on the bottom. She had a crushed velvet long sleeve shirt with a black vest over the top. Her black boots had pointy toes and her hair was long, grey, and wild, flying about her. She didn't wear makeup and her skin was wrinkled but still somehow looked healthy and supple. Her eyes were still bright, purple and gold, they told of her intelligence. She was old but she hadn't lost her mind.

"Why have you come here, Carine, and why have you brought a Magician?" The woman's voice was cracked as she spoke, telling of her age.

"She needs a favor."

"I am not inclined to do favors for Magicians passing through town."

I stepped forward before she could go back in the house. "Please, Celeste. I am Fawn Malero, my father is the leader of the Seattle area and I keep order over a small part of the city. I need your help and my problem concerns all supernaturals."

"I'm listening."

"There is a Magician who has been selling magical items to humans."

Celeste's eyes flashed and I knew we had her. "What do you need me for?"

"We have a sting operation of sorts set up, but we need a tracer spell put on the money."

"Simple."

"Thank you I—"

She held up a hand, cutting me off. "If I do this for you, I expect something in return."

"Of course, what do you need?"

"I need you to deliver a message to Misty."

I was taken aback. "Misty?" I said noncommittally.

"Yes, these are my terms."

She wasn't going to pretend I might not know who she was referring to. "I will deliver a message." And hopefully it wouldn't piss Misty off.

"Would you like to come in for some tea?"

"No!" Carine and I both said in unison.

"We really are in a bit of a time crunch. We'll return for you at sunset," Carine said, already backing away. I wondered what kind of experience Carine had had with a Witch's helpful tea.

"I can get myself to your house."

"Fine then, see you at sunset." Relief was clear in Carine's voice.

"Thank you, Celeste," I said and hurried back to the car. "So, what kind of helpful tea have you been given?"

Carine laughed bitterly. "I wanted a baby, so I came to Celeste for a potion that would help me feel good about mating with a Werewolf male, just for baby making purposes. It made me so horny I must have made my way through the whole northern pack before it wore off. It was humiliating and I didn't even conceive so it was a wasted humiliation. That was before I met Jax, now I am content with our life."

That was heavy and I didn't know what to say so I didn't say anything.

"What's your tea story?"

I blushed. "Nothing compared to yours, I must admit. I drank some clarity tea, without knowing. I was deep in denial about liking Logan at the time and oh man, I was like a cat in heat when I saw him next. Luckily it didn't last long." I felt dumb for even caring about it now. I hadn't even slept with Logan under its influence.

"Yeah, mine wins," Carine laughed.

We arrived back at the house near sunset, Logan was back with the cash, and he had pulled the shackles out of his bag. Jax was admiring them.

"You mean *nothing* can escape these?"

"Nothing that we know of," I said proudly. "My father forged them himself, its one of his talents."

"Amazing... I wouldn't mind a set for play." Jax's eyes flashed, and a seductive grin lifted her lips.

Visions of Jax dominating more than just some poor human man flashed through my mind and I couldn't look at Carine as my face heated. "Perhaps as a thank you, we could send some your way."

"That would be delightful." Jax handed the shackles back to Logan.

"Are we good to go with the tracking spell?" Logan asked, carefully sticking the shackles into his belt at his back where his jacket would easily hide them.

"Yes, Celeste will be here at sunset, she'll spell the money."

"Then I will take it and collect the human. He will go directly to the bar and wait. He will bring the trinket back to his place and wait for me to collect it and give him his reward.

I shivered at the way she said reward and I wondered at Carine's acceptance of the obviously sexual relationship between Jax and this human, even if there was no intercourse technically there was still penetration.

We all took the next hour to relax and prepare ourselves for the coming nights adventures.

"How long have they been together?"

"Carine and Jax?"

"Yeah, their relationship is interesting."

"Yes, I agree. They've been at it for a long time though and they've accepted each other for who they are. I think they are one of the most solid couples I know to be honest. I would put my money on them over Drake and Zin, or Betina and Tony. There's a maturity to their acceptance, they have rules, believe me, set in stone and they don't break them."

I thought about this, a mature relationship so Jax could feed on humans and dominate at least one in a way that no doubt was very sexual to the human. What was Carine's little secret I wondered. Maybe she still had sex with male Werewolves from time to time. I thought back to her story about the tea, it hadn't seemed as though she'd enjoyed the sexual experience. So, it must be something else. Of course, it was none of my business. Then I remembered the twins last night. I had seen a familiarness between them and Jax on the couch early on, and later I'd caught Carine staring at them lustfully and giving one a very familiar pat on the bottom. So maybe that's where Carine's exceptions lay.

"You look thoughtful."

My face blazed, "I was just thinking of using those shackles on you," I lied. Logan growled and pounced. I quickly found myself in those very shackles.

When the sun was going down we met in the kitchen and Celeste showed up at the moment the house's blinds automatically went up. She was punctual but she didn't seem happy to be here. She went about the kitchen brewing tea without talking to anyone. It smelled terrible.

"This spell will leave a purple trail seen only by those who drink this," Celeste poured the tea into four cups.

I met Carine's eyes across the table. "Cheers." We all lifted the cups and threw back the warm liquid like a shot. It tasted like cinnamon, not bad. I didn't feel any affects right away, that was comforting. I looked at Logan, normal lust, I looked at Jax and Carine, just an appreciation for a beautiful form. My eyes landed on the money; it was surrounded by a deep purple haze. "Woah."

"Oh good, I'm not the only one who sees it," Logan said.

"That should trail behind the money for at least thirty minutes before disappearing. You should have no trouble following it right to your man," Celeste said.

"Thank you, Celeste, you have no idea how glad I am that you could do this for us."

Celeste just harrumphed, reminding me of Evie and I felt a moment of homesickness. "Tell my daughter I want to see her."

"What?"

"Misty," she said and hurried away before I could ask any more questions.

"If Misty is her *daughter!* She is hella old!" I gasped.

"I told you," Carine said.

"I wonder if she knows she's a grandmother," Logan asked quietly, as if she might still be close enough to hear.

"Aww," Carine said dramatically.

Jax picked up the money. "I will meet you as soon as the human has the money and is headed for the bar." She kissed Carine and left.

It was amazing how well the spell worked, there was a hazy purple line that went from the table and out the door where Jax had gone. "I guess it works."

"Awesome! Let's go get into position," Logan said.

We drove to the main city strip. Mr. S was meeting our human at a crowded bar. He was going by the name Bill because that's what Logan had used

216

when he put the question on the message board. The bar was located in the bottom floor of a large brick building and across the street was another large brick building. We planned to hang out on the roof across the street and keep a distant eye on things. It was cold, but it was the best plan we had. It would allow for a quick pursuit once Stefan left the bar.

As we watched, it was easy to see the human was in the bar waiting alone. I was able to examine him a bit and was happy at the perfection of the pick. He looked like a sad sort of lonely human. Not tall, a bit on the thin side, glasses, and short brown hair. He was wearing a long sleeve button up flannel shirt and khaki pants. I couldn't tell what his shoes looked like, but I wouldn't be surprised to find they were a brand new pair of white tennis shoes. I struggled with human years but if I had to guess, I would say he was between forty and fifty. There was nothing remarkable about him and he was definitely not about to start attracting the females around him. He shifted a bit nervously and sipped a glass of white wine. "He's perfect."

"I don't think we could have done better," Logan agreed.

"He is very excited to be doing me a favor," Jax smiled meaningfully and licked her lips.

I shivered and turned back to the bar. Logan thought I was cold and put an arm around me. We waited and watched for an hour before noticing someone walk down the street. A human wasn't likely to notice anything different about him, he just looked like a confident man, but there was more to it. He walked as if he were in charge here, better than the humans around him and he was very much on a mission. He wore all black and even from here I could tell he had on a gaudy amount of silver jewelry; Magicians were always a little flashy. His eyes swept constantly around looking for danger and thankfully that never extended up. He was nervous about this meeting, and I hoped we weren't going to blow it by being this close. He stopped a few feet from the bar and stared inside, he seemed to spot our human who had his back to him. He stared for way too long, I was sure something was wrong, maybe he could sense the spell. Maybe he knew this guy somehow, knew his name wasn't Bill! "Shit," I hissed as he turned and walked away from the entrance then turned sharply disappearing between buildings.

"Don't give up yet, he's being cautious is all. There is a back entrance to the bar, maybe he just wants to get closer to Bill without being seen just yet." Carine's reassurance was of little comfort when we didn't see anyone join Bill for the next fifteen minutes.

A waitress appeared at Bills table and handed him something, his tab probably. He looked at it and then hurried to pay and leave. "Something's wrong," Jax said. "His instructions were clear; he was not to leave without the exchange taking place." Her tone was harsh, and I wondered what a punishment from her would entail.

I shivered again. "What do we do?"

Jax looked at her phone. "He is meeting Mr. S on the trails of Tubbs Hill. Something must have spooked him, he's testing. I bet he's close, watching to see if anyone follows the human."

I was worried, if he got spooked and ran, we were never going to be able to trick him again. "What do we do?"

"We wait. We know we can follow the money; we don't need to see the exchange. In a couple minutes we will split up to watch both exits off the hill from a distance. When we see the spell, we close in and follow, grab when it's safe." Logan's plan seemed reasonable, and he'd been on the hill this morning so he no doubt had a good idea of it working, but I worried.

We waited thirty minutes before taking up positions at the entrances. One was near Carine and Jax's house, coming out in a neighborhood. We thought this was his likely exit point because it would be easy to get lost among the streets and houses. The other exit was an open field across from a park and next to a small marina, which seemed less likely. Logan and Jax took the more likely street side exit and Carine and I watched the field side. We didn't have the shackles with us so if we spotted him we had to get Logan and Jax over to us, we were mostly just going to be watching. I was pretty good with this plan; I had no interest in trying to take down Stefan by myself. I knew he could influence through touch, and he could levitate things, it was likely he had other talents too that we didn't know.

We watched for a while then Carine got a message. Jax had received a message from the human, the exchange had been made but he didn't know where the man had gone, he'd blacked out apparently, so we had no idea which side he was going to come out. We watched and waited and nothing, then I saw a movement, a dark shape in the shadows and a faint purple haze. "Shit, text Jax." I didn't wait, I slunk closer as he turned sharply at the end of the trail and went toward the water. This wasn't what we had expected. He disappeared behind a small building, and I took the opportunity to run closer, something told me I didn't want him to get far. I pressed myself against the building, some kind of snack shack I assumed, and listened. I couldn't hear anything so I slunk around, I wasn't sure where Carine had gone, but I couldn't wait. I did my best spy imitation, peeking around a corner, saw nothing and slunk along another wall. I spotted Logan and Jax across the field headed this way as fast as they could without being noticed. When I got to the next corner I did a quick peek, there were docks, boats and something shadowed making its way down there with a purple haze following. My heart sped up and I knew he was going to get on a boat, and we were going to lose him. I had no options. Before I could think about what I was doing I dropped to the ground and crawled around the corner keeping as close to the shadow of the building and ground as I could. I heard a nearby splash and saw the shadow freeze for a moment, look around nervously then hurry his steps. *Damnit!*

I slid on my belly down a small embankment and into the water, it was freezing and if I weren't full of adrenaline I would probably already be chattering. I saw something move through the water near me. A large white wolf, Carine! She must have been the splash. We had the same idea it seemed. She'd gone up the trail and undressed then shifted and jumped in. It was impossible to tell from here which boat he might be headed to. Carine was a fast swimmer but her white coat glistened in the moonlight. She had to stick to shadows as much as she could and was getting nowhere fast. I reached a dock quickly and peeked over, he was bent down on the next dock over, untying a boat I assumed. I looked at Carine and pointed, she ducked under the water and went under the dock, I followed as best I could, but the cold was starting to get to me. I could feel my fingers and toes numb, my hips ached suddenly, and I thought for a second this was how I was going to die. A terrible cold death! It couldn't get much worse than that!

I felt a pull on my wrists and my body propelled through the water under the dock and out the other side, I came out of the water with too much noise I was certain, gasping for air but I didn't care in that moment. Grey hair appeared to float beside me and then lifted, a beautiful pale face appeared next. *Fiona,* I mouthed and she winked then motioned her head to where Stefan was. He must have froze when I broke through the water, I heard him now though and he was walking this way, *shit*!

Fiona clapped a hand over my mouth and pulled me under the water. It was creepy, the way she completely disappeared under there, but I could distinctly feel her hand on my mouth. My lungs

221

started to burn but she held me tight, it wasn't safe, I knew that's what she was indicating but if I drowned then what was the use of all this? Then I felt her lips on mine and she was pushing air into my lungs. I was okay, for the moment. She let me up slowly, this time I didn't splash and gasp. We made our way over to the other dock and I risked lifting my head up enough to see him. He was no more then three feet from me, but what could I do? I didn't have the shackles and I couldn't very well say *stop in the name of the law*...

Fiona didn't seem to understand that though because there was a sudden rush and I was flying on a spout of water, up and over and right into the very surprised body of Stefan. His eyes were wide, his mouth gaping and he didn't react, he was so shocked. I had crashed into him along with a couple hundred gallons of water. He was knocked down and I was straddling him, soaking wet and just as shocked as he was.

"Fawn?" He gasped, thankfully still too shocked to make a move to get out from under me.

"You're under arrest," I gasped poking my finger into his chest.

He smiled wickedly, realizing what was happening. He grabbed my hips throwing me off of him and jumping into the boat. I landed hard on my back; I would have some new bruises. I saw a flash of white as Carine crawled out of the water and jumped onto Stefan in the boat. She knocked him down and had her jaws around his neck by the time I scrambled to my feet. I could hear Logan and Jax pounding down the dock to us now, no more reason to hide.

"Like I said, you're under arrest, Stefan. For selling magical items to humans. What the hell is wrong with you?" I panted.

Carine levitated then, right off of Stefan and dropped into the water. He jumped to the key in the ignition, and I leaped onto his back as he started it. "Get off me, bitch!" He yelled and I felt myself lift and landed in the water again. The boat had started but Logan and Jax were there, both leaping into the boat at the same time. I watched in horror as the boat rushed back, taking out half the dock and wedged itself right up on top of another smaller boat. Logan was the first to recover it seemed, popping up and then falling forward, I saw a flash of silver as he moved, he had the shackles ready!

"Do you need assistance again?" Fiona's voice surprised me; she was right beside me.

"I think I can handle it." I swam to the dock and lifted myself out. Carine was next to me, naked and human now. Barely even wet!

"That was fun!" she said brightly.

I could only chatter, I was sure hypothermia was setting in, maybe frostbite. Logan was soon beside us, dragging a body. "Is he dead?" I asked a little hopeful.

"Just knocked out, he hit his head when the boat crashed." Logan looked at me thoroughly, eyes narrowed. "Are you hurt?" He growled.

"Just cold mostly, a little bruised I'm sure."

"I can get her back to the house fast," Fiona said, she was floating half out of the water now, amazingly dry from the waist up.

"I'll meet you there with this," Logan said, kicking Stefan lightly. Stefan groaned, starting to wake up. "Is that okay with you?" Logan looked at me doubtfully.

"Whatever gets me warm and dry the fastest." Logan leaned down and kissed me, I scooted to the edge of the dock and Fiona scooped me up into her arms and sunk into the water. Amazingly my body was unaffected by the cold water as she held me close.

Jax scooped up Carine. "We'll beat you there," she said with a wink and took off running, Vampires were very fast. Fiona sunk down until only our heads were above the water then started moving, gliding through the water at an incredible speed. The wind chilled my face, but my body remained neutral. It was a peaceful experience, the moon, and stars bright above us and reflecting in the dark calm water. There were no humans about as we rounded the hill and headed toward the small stretch of beach we'd been at last night.

She carried me all the way to the house. Jax was at the door before we got there holding it open and offering towels. I accepted them gratefully. "Thank you, Fiona, for all your help." I chattered as I wrapped myself tight. Without her magic I was feeling all the cold wetness now.

"Of course! Now you better get yourself into a warm bath."

I wanted nothing more but didn't want to miss Logan getting back. Carine was wrapped in a blanket near the fireplace and Jax was working on lighting it. I moved close, ready for the heat too. There was a lot of noise at the back door and Logan dragged Stephan in, dropping him in the mudroom. He crossed the house quickly and pulled me in for a very welcome warm embrace. "Why aren't you upstairs in a hot shower?"

"I wanted to make sure you made it back."

He growled and picked me up, walking to the stairs. "I'll be right back for that garbage." He called behind him as he carried me up. He set me down in the bathroom and undressed me quickly, started the shower, then turned me around to examine my backside. He touched it gently, but I tensed. "You've got quite the bruise forming already."

"Yeah, I think the cold was keeping me from feeling it." I was starting to really ache all over my lower back. "But it was worth it! I am so happy we stopped him." I met Logan's eyes in the mirror, he was frowning. I cocked my head to the side, silently questioning.

"This is too dangerous an occupation, Fawn."

I pursed my lips and raised an eyebrow. "Because I'm a girl?"

"No, because you're a Magician with no defensive abilities and—"

"And I'm weak like a human girl." I cut him off and spun around, then pushed him out of the bathroom and closed the door. Then locked it for good measure and stepped into the hot shower. *Asshole!*

I was still mad when I got out of the shower, so I was happy to see Logan hadn't returned to the bedroom. I made a quick phone call to tell my father the result of our little sting operation and tell him to be ready for Stefan tomorrow. Then I fell asleep, exhausted, and sore, both physically and emotionally. How could Logan not think I could handle this job, I had created this job!

Chapter 20

After saying our goodbyes in the early morning and gagging Stefan, he wouldn't stop talking! We were on our way back to Seattle. I was a little sad to leave the quiet city and did hope I could visit again sometime. Logan and I hadn't spoken about what occurred in the bathroom. What was the point? I knew where he stood, and he knew where I stood and they were opposite ends. It felt useless. The worst part was that although I didn't feel like I was helpless without him, I did realize he played an important role in my ability to move through and understand the supernatural world. I just wasn't as worldly as he was, but I could get there if I had to.

The ride was silent and uncomfortable.

We went straight to my parent's house to deposit Stefan. My father met us outside. "I can't believe Stefan was selling magical items to humans!"

"Yeah, I guess you can't blame me now for not wanting to date him," I said snarkily. My father gave me a chastising look and my mother patted his arm.

"We never would have let him stay with us, had we known," she said softly.

"I know, sometimes people aren't what they seem."

"Where do you want him?" Logan asked, lifting him out of the back seat and throwing him over his shoulder. Still gagged and shackled Stefan could only grunt, but he could have walked, this was just more demeaning and I think that's what Logan was going for.

"In the basement, shut him in the third cell. I will go down and release his shackles later."

Logan went into the house and my father turned to me. "Fawn, what were you thinking? Stefan is obviously dangerous, and you could have been seriously hurt! Or worse!"

I rolled my eyes. "I am not a fragile flower; I am a grown woman and if this is what I want to do with my life then this is what I will do!" Why the hell was everyone always thinking they knew what's best for me!

My mother touched my arm and I instantly calmed, she had the ability to affect your emotions if she touched you, subtle but effective. "Fawn, you know we just want what's best for you. Logan is... dangerous and this mess he's got you involved in is just too much."

I pulled away, breaking the effect. "*I* chose this, Logan or not I am in the business of taking care of things supernatural. I will continue to help because it's what makes me feel useful and happy. For once in my life, I am happy with what I am and where I am."

Logan caught my rant and I saw a guilty look cross his features before he covered it with determination. "When can we expect his trial?" Logan strode over to me and even though I was mad at him, I was thankful for the show of support.

"I will speak with him shortly and let you know. If he wants a trial, we should be able to provide that tomorrow night, if he wants to forgo the embarrassment..." My father trailed off and I knew what he meant. Death would be the proper punishment for this sort of betrayal to the supernatural community. His guilt was doubtless, and the trial would be shameful for his family.

"Oh, don't forget this." I handed my father a small gold bottle with an elegant A made of rubies on the front.

"Aphrodite's perfume," he gasped.

"I guess so."

"This would be very dangerous in human hands," he said and looked at me with a bit of grudging respect.

I hugged my mother goodbye and we left.

"I'm sorry," Logan said softly.

I was sure I didn't hear him right. "What?"

Logan cleared his throat. "I'm sorry. I should never have tried to get you to quit investigating. I worry about you because I care for you deeply. I would never ask you to do anything that would make you unhappy. Even if it would keep you safe."

I unbuckled and scooted close to him, wrapping my arms around him. He put one arm around me and pulled me closer. I laid my face against his chest, and he kissed the top of my head. "Thank you. Honestly, I would have a much harder time without you, though I could do it, and I would."

"I know," he said, and I felt his chest rumble with laughter. I was pretty certain he still doubted my ability but that's okay, I would continue to prove myself to him and everyone else. "So will you put the necklace back on?"

I gasped and reached for my neck. "Oh, Logan I think I've lost it! It must have fallen off in the struggle with Stefan or in the water!"

Logan just sighed and patted my leg. "I thought you threw it out on purpose, getting ready to kick me to the curb for good finally."

I laughed, "That won't be happening any time soon."

When we got to my house there was a vehicle I didn't recognize outside. "Betina has a guest?"

"Probably Tony," Logan growled.

"I thought you liked him."

"I do, but that doesn't mean I trust him, he's a young male."

"Oh!" I caught his drift. "Well lets just make sure we make a lot of noise going inside." The last thing I wanted to do was catch them in the act on the couch. We dropped and jiggled the keys at the front door, and I even loudly pronounced, "I am so glad to be home!" before opening the door. It wasn't necessary. Betina, Tony and Annabel were sitting around the kitchen table looking at us like we were nuts as we walked in. Evie was hovering in the kitchen and even the animals were looking curiously at us. "Hi," I said carefully.

"Welcome home," Evie said. "Your animals missed you."

As if on cue Jasper and Sofia walked in meowing demanding *food!* Jake and Pete yipped happily and rushed Logan. Chester tweeted and landed on my shoulder, at least he was always happy to see me. "Tony, it's nice to see you again, and Annabel! I am so happy you're back on land." I hurried over and gave her a hug.

"I just got back this morning actually." Her eyes lit up and I couldn't wait to hear all the details. "Tony was nice enough to give me a lift."

"Have you been home to see your mother?"

"Yes, she was getting worried, I think if I'd been gone another day, she would have sent my father out to look for me."

"Yikes!" It was serious if Misty was going to talk to Fanlin about anything.

"Yeah, so I guess it's good I returned. Though I am sad I missed your adventure!"

"Was your trip successful?" Betina asked.

"Yes, very. How were things here and the studio?"

"All fine, though I think if you don't start teaching some of your classes you might lose clients, they think you've given up on them."

I rolled my eyes; humans were so sensitive. "I will work all day tomorrow."

"And Stefan?" Annabel pressed.

"He's at my parent's house, my father will question him and determine if a trial is wanted."

"He may just accept punishment?" Annabel asked, surprised.

"It's likely," Logan responded. "A trial can be embarrassing for the family."

I needed a distraction, so I cleaned the kitchen and made an early dinner for everyone whether they wanted it or not. Betina and Tony went out after that and Annabel went home to tell her mother that Celeste had sent her a message, she wants to see her. I was guiltily happy that I wasn't the one who actually had to give the message and I didn't tell Annabel who Celeste was, that wasn't really my place. My father called with the expected news that Stefan was forgoing a trial and accepting punishment. I was glad I wasn't going to have to see his arrogant face again, but still sad for his family, he had two sisters, a nephew, and a mother he was going to leave behind.

Logan cuddled me on the couch, and we watched movies for the rest of the night. Romantic comedies, nothing heavy. After the second one, I turned to Logan with as serious a face as I could muster. "Are you afraid you're next?"

"Next for what?"

"Well, this is the second man who I kind of dated that my father's had to put to death."

Logan raised an eyebrow and looked thoughtful. "Worth the risk," he said simply then leaned down and kissed me passionately.

We were just about to take ourselves upstairs when there was a very firm knock on the door. I looked at Logan and frowned. Most people who came over no longer knocked, we were past those pleasantries. Which meant this was likely an unknown. "Wait here," I commanded and walked to the door. I felt Logan close behind me, obviously he wasn't going to listen.

"Human," Logan said sniffing deep.

"Probably a neighbor needs to borrow sugar." I opened the door, nervous. A police officer stood there, and my mind flew to Betina and Tony. "Oh my god is everyone okay?"

"Yes ma'am, I am here to speak with Fawn Malero, that you?" He had dark hair and eyes, short and round body and his accent was from somewhere way east.

I sensed nothing but human from him and I was very confused. "Yes, that's me."

"I suppose you know that Ben Benson was moved to a psychiatric facility last week, to undergo testing before his trial."

"No but I guess I'm not surprised."

"Well, ma'am he escaped last night, and we are afraid he might try to contact you." His eyes narrowed and he tried to look past me into the house. "He *hasn't* tried to contact you, has he?"

"No, of course not, why would he?"

"Well you visited him, and he just never stopped talking about you, to anyone who would listen. I'm afraid he's been quite obsessed."

My heart stopped and my mouth gaped, I couldn't move or think. Logan stepped forward and pulled me close to him. "Should we be worried?"

"Just aware, and let the police know if you see or hear anything, anything at all that seems suspicious or out of place. We will find him, don't worry."

"Thank you, Sir," Logan said, I still couldn't speak. The officer left and Logan guided me over to the couch. "Fawn are you okay?"

I looked at him, fairly sure I wasn't. "How?"

"I was worried that day when you talked about the glass between you. Was there anything else between you two that could have interfered with the spell?"

"Glasses!" I suddenly remembered. "He was wearing glasses too, oh Logan I was dripping sensuality for him, it was the only way to get him to talk."

Logan growled. "I'll call the boys, you won't be alone or unguarded until the psycho's found, and if we find him before the cops... there won't be any need to call them."

The look of murder in Logan's eyes was at the same time terrifying and completely endearing, he loved me. I smiled and pulled him in for a kiss then ran, making him chase me up to the bedroom, it was one of his favorite games. Calling in the armed guards could wait.

About The Author

Courtney Davis is a mother, wife and teacher who has always loved to find time to escape into a good story. She's been in love with reading and writing since she was a child and dreams of a life where she can devote herself fully to creating worlds and exploring relationships. To give someone else enjoyment through her words is the ultimate thrill.

Lansford Guy
THE GUARDIANS

Wayne E. & Sean P. Haley
AN APOLOGY TO LUCIFER

David Kruh
INSEPARABLE

Shawn Mackey
THIS WORLD OF LOVE AND STRIFE

Jeanne Matthews
DEVIL BY THE TAIL

C.K. McDonough
STOKING HOPE

Fidelis O. Mkparu
SOULFUL RETURN *(Nov 2022)*

Phillip Otts
A STORM BEFORE THE WAR
THE SOUL OF A STRANGER
THE PRICE OF BETRAYAL

Erika Rummel
THE INQUISITOR'S NIECE
THE ROAD TO GESUALDO
EVITA AND ME

Vanessa Ryan
THE TROUBLE WITH MURDER

J. M. Stephen
NOD
INTO THE FAIRY FOREST
RISE OF THE HIDDEN PRINCE
SILENCE AND RUPTURED WATERS
THE RISE OF RUNES AND SHIELDS

Jessica Stilling
THE WEARY GOD OF ANCIENT TRAVELERS
BETWEEN BEFORE AND AFTER (*Nov 2022*)
AFTER THE BARRICADES (*May 2023*)

Claryn Vaile
GHOST TOUR

Felicia Watson
WHERE THE ALLEGHENY MEETS THE MONONGAHELA
WE HAVE MET THE ENEMY
SPOOKY ACTION AT A DISTANCE
THE RISKS OF DEAD RECKONING
WHERE NO ONE WILL SEE (*Apr 2023*)

Daniel A. Willis
IMMORTAL BETRAYAL
IMMORTAL DUPLICITY
IMMORTAL REVELATION
PROPHECY OF THE AWAKENING
FARHI AND THE CRYSTAL DOME
VICTORIA II
THE CHILDREN OF VICTORIA II

Joyce Yarrow
SANDSTORM

238